THE HUMAN SKILLS

LEVI SEYLER

Contents

1

INTRODUCTION

Depending on what part of the globe humanity lives on, a percentage of 1 to 6 percent of Neanderthal DNA lies in our genome. In Africa, Southeast Asian and Pacific Islander populations can be less, if at all. The point I am making — is for modern humans to have any amount of early man genes in them, is proof that small groups of different humans competitively shared their lives — maybe for pure survival. There was a strong reason to live in small groups, but when more work together like hunting, more food could be eaten. The ancient lost civilizations archaeologists are digging up, they too live in small groups for many reasons. As they came together, small groups became tribes. To this very day, humanity has found ways to collect themselves for a better life. This is called Interpersonal Intelligence — social skills.

Before you say it, Neanderthals were more intelligent than we were told in public school. In an article written on July 9, 2013, Did Neanderthals have language? "A recent study suggests that Neanderthals shared speech and language with modern humans"

Using a language is part of the social structure. We can easily see how strange it was for them to see Cro-Magnon for the very first time. Yes, they were in an anatomical position as they were, but they were a complete genetic set of humanity. Today, we are diverse in many cultures and ways of life, which still scares people today. The Republican Party is illegally dividing the LGBTQIA people. I can't say that we are losing our Interpersonal Intelligence, but we can do a much better job at it. Because the news media makes things worse, it does not mean our society is falling apart or losing all perspectives of reality. It could easily mean, we have already approached a new era that is getting us to see a new and fresh perspective of reality itself.

Having a better life does not mean things are ideally perfect or horrible. Let me pause for a moment and share two words with you — utopia and dystopia. The first word comes from two Greek words, UO, meaning not, and TOPOS, meaning place. This means, there is no such thing as an ideal society. Regarding the second word, DYS means bad. I have to admit, the Ukrainians are living in dire straits as Russia's government is bombing the <BLEEP> out of them, but they are fighting back. This means they will see daylight because Putin is losing this war. We survived as the world went through WWI through the Cold War (which was not cold at all). With around 50 years between 1945 and 1991, this war lasted 45-6 years. Maybe why NATO and the rest are slow in getting directly involved in this Ukrainian mess. As this story is concerned, humanity will see the light of day because we live through a hot 77 years of war (1914 - 1991). My point, looking at a small dark moment in life does not mean it is the end of the world. A pleasant moment is not bad in itself — unless people, as a whole (living in their comfort zones for too long) they cannot get out of the rut they made themselves.

When larger groups live together, it usually means more and new challenges — the good, the bad, and the outright ugly. Where would humanity be today if it were not for everyone taking the necessary risks to advance? In the 21st century, many advances have allowed us to populate the world with nearly 8 billion people. Overall, we are healthy and learned so much over the decades. It was over thousands of years from the first early settlement to how we live today. Our technical advancements over the decades have excelled us faster than most have realized.

With the radio, we could hear what was going on around the world during the World Wars, hear music, have stories told, and all the rest. Later, we had movies, television, and other forms of communication for millions to witness. Today, through the Internet, we can talk and see family and friends at all points of the world in real-time as if we were in the same room or area.

ARPAnet was formed in late 1966; it took 24 years for us to have the Internet publicly. Social media was formed in early 2001. From statista.com, "As of January 2021, there were 4.66 billion active Internet users worldwide - 59.5 percent of the global population. Of this total, 92.6 percent (4.32 billion) accessed the Internet via mobile devices." We have been a collective consciousness since nearly day one of human existence — from the Neanderthals to our modern technologies. That is why humanity has advanced technically since the early 70s — the birth of the microchip. The integrated circuit was created much earlier — on Sept. 12, 1958. Humanity wants to evolve the means of collecting themselves more and more. This is what is called, Collective Consciousness or hive mind. From a TEDx Video, Imagining the Future: The Transformation of Humanity | Peter Diamandis | TEDxLA (https://www.youtube.com/watch?v= 7XrbzlR9Qml), we could have a human hive mind in our lifetime.

As I have proven, there is no such thing as a utopia or dystopia. When we read novels, watch television shows or movies regarding such things, we experience a collective — a large portion of humanity turning into mindless puppets. Yes, nations of humans have been in a war that many suffer. The losers usually become slaves to the victors if the government leader is a tyrant. From the Stone Age to our modern age, no one has been turned into a mindless drone through many technological advancements. What does this mean if we are not drones to some queen or the like?

When done right, one day, human beings will have technical implants in their bodies to enhance themselves and will be able to communicate with others by the use of our minds. If that is too horrifying to you in the enhancement of humanity, don't people wear glasses to see better, or hearing aids to hear better from being hard of hearing? Dr. Stephen Hawking had a computer chip in his body to be able to communicate with the world around him. Many others had implants to better their lives. Dr. Hawking or the others were not turned into mental slaves of the ones who created these technologies.

The worse that has come out of social media and new Internet technologies is misinformation — but to a tiny degree. Not all of it is bad. When did fake news occur? That answer is easy to give — since the first time someone lied or misled others. There were endless wars in ancient times of civilization. Makes one wonder how humanity ever had the word civilized attached to them. Once again, there is no such thing as a perfect world. We will face horrible moments in human history, but they are only moments. Today, the Jews are alive and well even after facing one of the most horrifying Holocausts in the modern era.

If modern technology today could advance enough to allow the human mind to connect to a central network for all to share and experience thoughts, dreams, guidance, etc., then it will be gradual. As I wrote — the integrated circuit was created in 1958 and the microchip in the 70s. The first microcomputer was in the early 80s. These advancements may have appeared to be short, but the advancements were gradual — as all advancements are... to this very day.

2

CHAPTER 1

A young teenager by the name of Sophia Vitaloti, at the age of 17 had been connected to the hive mind at the age of nine. She was very intelligent before and realized her mind would not fry like a piece of bacon if she connected to a wonderful experience that nearly all around the world enjoyed.

Even though the whole planet, Earth was technically mentally connected as a central collective consciousness, it was not overnight. Throughout human existence, they have thrived over the millennium to socially connect. Now they have done so with advanced technology shortly after mapping the human mind. Scientists and other specialists have already mapped the human brain decades before. There is a huge difference between the mind and the brain.

The human race had nearly been a part of a collective consciousness since early man. Living in small groups made it possible to do things that could outright be impossible for individuals or a close group of five people to achieve. Over the centuries, civilized humans lived in tribes and cities of all sizes of humans living as a society. Patriotism was a giant proof that a collective was important to humanity as a whole. That did not stop as the years went onward.

In the technical age, there was the radio in early 1900. Around a decade later, television sprung into existence. Communicating and sharing ideas with the masses grew from there. Even though war is a horrible choice, sometimes it advances humanity soon after. The ARPAnet in late 1966 became the front-runner of a technical evolution the world had never experienced. What is called the Internet became public for the first time in 1990. Social media took off in 2001 and excelled beyond expectations.

Sophia lived in the year 2200. Be warned, over the years, humanity created a new perspective of measuring time. Before they could use their technologies to better themselves by having a huge hive mind through it, their attitudes had to be different from the past. It could be possible this number could be highly obscured. Time is more than linear.

There have been many that have not connected to this hive mind, and that concerned Sophia for some time.

Being a father, Nikolas could always tell when his daughter was overly concerned about things — even before she freely decided to connect to the hive.

Since the whole world wanted to do this through their technologies, they started with smaller hives and built things from there — which were the cities' hives connected to the State hive. Those hives were connected to the nation. Eventually, every nation was connected to everyone else. That means, there was not one major collective hub but the sharing of them no matter the size of the communities. Think of it as the ultimate INTERNET using liveware vs hardware and software.

This does not mean the old technologies were not used. It is hard to explain in mere words. One has to at some point experience something that is beyond the understanding of 21st-century life. A great deal has changed throughout the planet. I will let you explore those changes as you read onward. A narrator can only tell so much.

Later on that day, Sophia came to her father's study and sat in one of the three chairs provided. It did not have her name on it, but it was the one she always sat in. Her father did not say or do anything. He realized she had to initiate the conversation.

Since her father was a Greek Philosopher, both of them loved to discuss nearly everything, but this time it was something that concerned her since she had willfully connected to their hive. Seconds later, which felt like hours to her, she spoke in Greek, "Πατέρα, Έχω κάτι στο μυαλό μου. / Father, I have something on my mind." (Bampás means, father in Greek. Nikolas had no idea why she called him that. Before she was connected, she called him, daddy. She will call him Bampás even when they are talking in English. If you are wondering why she is talking in Greek, they did that a lot even before connecting with the hive.)

He still did not react to what she said by continually doing what he started before she walked in. Because they were both connected, he could feel her concerns more profoundly.

She continued, "Είμαι στη γωνία γιατί υπάρχουν πολλοί που δεν έχουν επιλέξει να συνδεθούν με την κυψέλη μας. Ο εγκέφαλός μας δεν έχει καταστραφεί, κανείς δεν μας ελέγχει και η ζωή πριν συνεχίζεται καθώς αυτό το τεχνικό θαύμα δεν υπήρξε ποτέ. / I am cornered why there are a good many that have not chosen to be connected to our hive. Our brains have not been destroyed, no one is controlling us, and life before is continuing as this technical marvel never existed."

Since he was not doing anything important, he closed the book as he normally would and quietly walked to his chair and sat down. He said in English with a slight Greek accent, "How many do you think are not connected, my dear daughter."

Because the world had been connected as a shared collective mind, racism and other social hatreds quickly evaporated as they should have never started to begin with. Nikolas met his future wife, Pippa Gill (Gill was her maiden name), at a big library in England, where she worked. She was, at that time, one of the head caretakers. She was so proficient at her job, everyone looked up to her — including the government.

She huffed and answered, "I have no way of knowing the exact number, but I say far too many."

He thought over what he wanted to ask her, "Did you change when you freely connected to what these individuals think as controversial?"

She was about to get furious at him for suggesting such a word but stopped herself. It was something her father always did to her when examining things outside of her understanding. After calming her mind, "Bampás, it is not controversial to me. Why is it to them? All this was not done yesterday. If I understand right..."

He gently interrupted, "Exactly my point, my daughter." He paused for a brief moment and continued, "before you can find the answers you seek, you need to study every aspect of the people in question cultures. Believe me, there are more diversities to them than you may realize."

She thought quietly for a long moment, "If I am going to do this, I can't do this alone."

He smiled, "That my daughter is an understatement. In every discipline in life, one has to get help. No scientist or philosopher did things alone. Forget the movies and television shows. They have a protagonist in them, but no living soul can learn what the story had set them out to do, alone." He paused once again, "your mother works at the library. She can help you gather the basics you need to build a foundation on how to begin answering the question you gave me."

"I have tried to find the answers by meditating in the hive collective, but I learned nothing."

"That my dear is why you have failed. You don't know what questions to ask. I gave you a question in return to yours because the number of those who have not decided to connect to our hive mind system is never the issue. The Hive is not a library or any other knowledge repository. I believe you will need to learn the history of this technical wonder before you can find what you are looking for."

She smiled, I see why you are a philosopher. The discipline you have is the only way to learn."

"Know this if anything you can learn from me, 'Philosophy of science without history of science is empty; history of science without philosophy of science is blind.' You must use every resource at your disposal to achieve the goals you have in your life. In all the years of knowing you, my precious daughter, you have never been empty-handed or blind, but for you to learn what you have set yourself to do, you will walk into the unknown. Knowledge is an ongoing process."

She smiled again, "It is also in constant change. When I was initially connected to our local hive hub, I realized I should have done so earlier. I don't regret doing so that day, but how much I have experienced in the initial moment."

"Believe it or not, Sophia, all that came from you. Trust me, knowledge is cold data. Without your experiences, you will never learn a single thing."

With a confused look, she asked, "Are you saying, this is easier to solve than I making it out to be?"

"Yes and no. A philosopher like myself has searched for the meaning of life, and we still have not found what we are looking for because life is always ongoing." He paused, "the ones that don't want to be connected to the hive mind have nothing to do with us. They have the right to choose as you did."

Trust me, Bampás, I am very much grateful to be a part of this wonder." She paused in thought, "I wonder if I am being biased?"

"Are you?"

"I don't feel that way."

"Let me put it to you this way, "Why would you care if they connect or not? There are no laws, medical reasons, or survival things. Once you find out why you are even curious, you will learn a whole lot more."

"Could it be fear? Are they afraid of something?"

"That is not the point. If you are a sociologist, then knowing the reasons may be beneficial. Are you one? Do you want to be such a professional?"

"It would be something to explore." She paused, "Why it upset me... could we, that have been connected, have done something wrong?"

He studied her quietly for a moment and realized there was something more. He threw it back at her, "Have you done something wrong when you first connected?"

She had already run through all her experiences before and after the blending of her mind with the local hive mind. It was several minutes later she felt the blending of the interconnection of all the other hives — including the nation's one. When her mind started to understand the minds all around the world, she did not know what to think. Their language and culture were marvelous but at that initial moment, she had little to no understanding of it all.

Because of Yeva Havrylivna Fesenko — a dear Ukrainian friend and Somova Angela Victorovna — a dear Russian friend, she understood their custom and the Russian language very well. She learned to speak a few languages — not because she was connected to the hive mind. She had the gift to learn different languages. If she was going to communicate with everyone around the world, she realized she could use her natural talents to do so. It was not the language itself. Language also teaches about the culture of that nation better than anything in the world. As Sophia's Bampás said, "A hive mind does not give you instant knowledge. Everyone had to go to school to learn.

"I have to admit, I don't know..."

"Stop right there! Admitting, I don't know is the key to learning. You don't need to necessarily explain yourself further."

"Are you suggesting..."

"Speculating will not answer your initial question. Because you are connected to the hive mind with billions of people does not give you the same knowledge, experiences, and all the rest automatically from the ones that were already connected."

"Yes, Bampás. I know. It was as if I had all their thoughts in my head but did not. Later I realized they were ghost memories or the like because they were not mine. Later, as I learned certain things, some of those experiences came back to me. I think they stuck with me especially as I continued to learn about those multitudes of experiences."

He smiled, "They were always there, Sophia. It was because you had nothing to connect with your mind — which has your thoughts, experiences, and all that makes you a unique person in the universe."

"So that is why you said, 'Philosophy of science without history of science is empty; history of science without philosophy of science is blind.' My mind was empty because I could not relate to either the philosophical aspect of the hive or the history of the people from another country." She paused for a moment, "so I am blinded by the question I asked you because I am in the same boat?"

With a big smile, "EXACTLY!"

****

The next day, it was Monday. It was back to school once again. Sophia got cleaned up that night. When she got out of her room to meet her mom, Pippa smiled at her, "Good morning my lovely daughter. How did you sleep?"

"I slept well. I usually do. At first, I thought it was because I was connected to the local hive mind, but after Bampás and I talked yesterday evening, I am learning there is more to this collective consciousness."

She smiled, "Trust me, I would not have done so myself if I could not be myself." She saw that look in her daughter's eyes. "yes, Sophia, we all had a choice. Most have joined their minds with everyone else, but they did not stop being themselves." Before giving her the chance to speak, "yes, baby, I monitored your mind as you were talking to your father."

"Why do some not join their minds with the rest?"

"First of all, it is for them to choose. I could have not done so if I was not 100% certain who I was before... can't be the same. Yes, I have changed over the years; we all do. I have heard from several, they just don't want to do so. Yes, some fear their minds will be invaded." She paused, "I don't blame them. Privacy means a great deal to some... more than others."

"I never felt violated even when I am undressing, taking a shower, etc."

"Even though it has been decades since the first time we have created such a marvel of allowing humanity to truly be a part of a collective consciousness, humanity has been working at it since early man."

"Yes, I have gotten bits and pieces of that from others, but it does not answer my question — why there are some that don't want to connect?"

"After setting the food on the table, she answered, "You said, you got information about the humanity of old wanting to collect themselves crudely as we have done with our collective hive network. It appears to me, baby, you need to learn a whole lot more."

As she was talking, Sophia helped put out the plates and eating utensils. When done, she asked, "I hope your library has this information."

All of a sudden a mental image — that the two ladies only saw — of her sociology instructor, Noda Miyu appeared. She was Japanese and living in the United States of America. She said to them both,

"I, too, have monitored your concerns, my young Sophia. I think you will need help with this if I may."

Sophia nodded because she realized she could see her actions as well as hear her.

"I have already changed my curriculum around it. The school's President agrees with this. There is more to know about why we have collected our minds than bettering ourselves as humans have done by collecting ourselves in a society of one sort or the other. This will be a project-based learning assignment."

Sophia smiled, "Thanks, Ms. Miyu. I am excited to see how this starts."

"Know this, '☒☒☒☒☒☒☒☒☒☒ (i no naka no kawazu taikai wo shirazu) English Translation: 'A frog in a well knows nothing of the sea.' This famous Japanese saying means someone sees the world through their limited perspective. They're quick to judge and think very big of themselves. It's used to remind someone that there are things bigger than them in the world. When this project is over, I hope you can see beyond the things that are bothering you regarding what you seek."

She replied in Japan-ese, "☒☒☒☒☒ ☒☒☒☒☒☒☒☒☒☒☒☒☒☒☒☒☒☒☒☒ ☒☒☒☒☒☒☒☒☒☒☒☒☒☒☒☒☒☒ (Arigatō. Anata ga ima itta koto wa ōku no koto o imi shimasu. Purojekuto o hajimeru no o tanoshi-minishiteimasu.) / Thank you. What you just said means a lot. I am looking forward to starting the project."

Ms. Miyu smiled, and she vanished.

It was not long before Nikolas was at the table. He was always at the table at the prompt time. It was to give the two lovely ladies a private moment together. For the rest of the morning, they talked as a family should as they ate breakfast.

****

It was not until after lunch Sophia's class with Ms. Miyu. If there was one class that was important after a planet full of human beings connected to a hive mind through technology, sociology would be it. There is more to learn about nations and ideologies all around the world. Learning about oneself is just as important. As Sophia has learned, to understand other people's minds on this hive network, it takes learning about oneself as a serious priority. Learning has everything to do with how our brain interprets the world around us in every detail.

When she entered the room Sophia said, "□□□□□ (Kon'nichiwa.) / Good afternoon."

Ms. Miyu smiled and replied in the same manner. She continued, "Your records have shown you have a great talent for learning languages. You pronounced Japanese very well."

"We had neighbors a while back who were Japanese."

"Don't cut yourself short. For a seventeen-year-old to learn as many languages over her life, that is very exceptional." She paused, "I take it by now, you realize what you know and have learned came from you — not your hive mind-melding."

"Yes, I have. I was more excited that it came from me than others. Yes, I have learned a great deal from the hive and the many minds I have associated with..."

"Learning and what has been shared with you are two entirely different things." She paused, "I am beginning to believe what you are concerned about is not how many have not mind-meld with the hive, but what would have happened to you if you did not."

She was amazed. She tried to keep that from entering the hive. "Bampás could not have known. How can she do so?" "I have to admit, I have that on my mind, but..."

She gave a reassuring smile, "I did not get it from you by our hive minds. It is all over your face and mannerisms. There is nothing wrong with how you have felt recently, think or whatever. Like there is nothing wrong with the masses that freely have not connected."

"If you are concerned that I want to be disconnected, please, believe me, I don't. I have fantasized about what would have occurred if I did not. Now knowing all I have become had nothing to do with joining billions of minds as one..."

"That is what you are not accepting. You have not changed because of whatever has been entering your life." She paused, "you did right, Sophia by joining the hive. I now believe you have a stronger desire to learn everything from the beginning, so you can excel in your life while being a part of this technical achievement we call, collective consciousness." Seeing more students quietly entering the room, she continued, "please, Sophia, have a seat. The class will start soon."

She replied, "ありがとう (Arigatō.) / Thank you" before sitting at a desk.

3

CHAPTER 2

It was not long until every student took their seat. After the bell rang, Noda Miyu stood up from her seat. She or any other instructor did not have to take the roll call of the students. Most if not all the students were hive connected. Some weren't; nevertheless, the reasons why it was easy to know which ones they were. It was not that the ones connected were telepathic. The instructors could use deductive reasoning to know who they were. After knowing such students on a personal level over the years, it was not hard to remember their names.

"My fellow students, I have a great curriculum for you this semester — thanks to a great suggestion by our fellow senior student, Sophia Vitaloti. This assignment is of several levels. The first one is the history of our hive-mind technology that several generations of us humans have been connected to, but it is so much more to it than you could ever realize. A male student about Sophia's age raised his hand. "Ms. Miyu replied, "If I remember right, your name is Zak Harris?"

He smiled, "Yes, ma'am." He paused, "I would like to know the history of collective consciousness in general."

She smiled, "I see you have an open mind. There is more to it than our technologies with collecting everyone's mind to our hive network."

"I never dive into anything before I know all the facts — all that I can get a hold of, I mean."

"An interesting idea; we should never do anything before learning all we can. Since Sophia will be the head leader of this project, I think you should take charge of the history of the human aspect." She deliberately did not mention the collective consciousness aspect. She was the type of instructor to give the initiative to the students.

With a confused look, "Please, pardon my confusion, but what does the history of humanity have to do with the hive mind all of you are connected to?"

"Believe it or not, the word collective consciousness has nothing to do with any technology. Over the many, many years, humanity had the drive to connect or collect themselves. That in itself is complex. I mean, it has different reasons and purposes. The major examples — which are too numerous to count alone... list — have slowly joined humanity in endless ways. We have cities, patriotism, many groups and ideas we share with others, and nations around the world."

He gave a surprising and strong interest to learn more about this topic. "In that case, thank you for giving me this task."

As Sophia was quietly sitting at her desk, listening to him with his mannerism, she started to have an interest in Zak. She started to become excited about this project that she would be leading. Seeing this, Ms. Miyu called her to face the class. "Do you have any other ideas?"

"Since this is a sociology class, maybe we need to come up with a questionnaire or the like."

The whole student body got excited, and they all showed it. Ms. Miyu turned on the large screen in front of the class and went to her desk. Her computer was already connected to it. She said, "This questionnaire should be done near the end. Why? There is a lot for everyone to learn, but we can start with some of the basics. It is obvious we should ask the willing participant, their name, gender, age..."

Sophia said, "We should ask about their national origin. Even though nearly every human mind is connected to their societal hive, and those are connected to bigger ones in the city, State, nations, and eventually the world, we are still individuals and have different customs in our special groups. Each one that will participate should be recognized as an individual rather than a hive mind. I, for one, am still an individual. As long as I am alive, I want to stay as such."

Ms. Miyu declared, "Well said! Yes, I am sure most if not all of us had our lives improved dramatically by being connected, but we function as individuals."

Zak said, "I get it! I remember reading civilized humans built on coming together for their survival and building a culture — over a slow process."

Still at her desk, the instructor said, "That is just a basic primer. It will be up to you and your team to gather more information." She looked at Sophia and back at him, "as you know, Ms. Vitaloti's mother works at our library. She would be the best to help you find things you may not realize exist."

A bit nervous, he said, "That will be helpful." He swallowed his emotions, "it is why I have not connected." He paused, "OH MY. I am nervous all of a sudden."

Already mind linked to the instructor, she suggested what they were contemplating over, "If I may, Zak — have you tried a temporal connection?"

"I can do that?"

Ms. Miyu smiled, "Yes, but may I give another suggestion." She waited for him to answer. After an enthusiastic nod, she continued, "learn more about the collective consciousness before taking such a leap."

He asked more cheerfully, "When or if I do so, how? I was never told I could do this on a temporal basis."

She looked at Sophia quietly once again and back at him. "If you like, Ms. Vitaloti can do that for you."

Sophia said, "When you are ready and not before, we can discuss how long you want to be connected. If you need more time, that process would be easy to do."

"If I may, and I hope I am not being rude, but how are you connected? I thought this process was some kind of surgical operation."

After a smile, Sophia said, "It will be the same as it was for all of us. Nanobots will be safely and painlessly injected into you. I will be happy to guide you along the way. New things will happen, but there will be nothing harmful or disturbing."

"How was it for you if you don't mind answering?"

She smiled again, to show everything will be alright, "I don't mind; it has been something unique for each one of us, so it can't be described in mere words. For me, it felt like I was hearing things, in my head, that was not there. It was a bit to take in, but after a time, it felt like all those minds guided me. With my own experiences, and everything that I have learned since I still feel them all guiding me. Trust me, Zak, I am nervous standing up here, but at the same time, I want to learn all I can as well."

"That makes sense. They understood what you were going through because they went through it themselves."

Sophia blurted out, "I am liking you every moment." After pulling her mind back on the project, she continued, "I will be happy to talk more about this out of class. If that is alright with you?"

"GREAT! Sure! I will be honored."

In her mind, Yeva, a Ukrainian friend, said, "Я бачу Софію Харріс у майбутньому. (YA bachu Sofiyu Kharris u may-butn'omu.) / I see a Sophia Harris in the future."

"Заткнись, дівчино! (Zatknys', divchyno!) / Shut the crap up, girl!"

"Не заперечувати; ти закохуєшся в нього. Мені не потрібно бути з тобою пов'язаним ментально, щоб побачити це. (Ne zaperechuvaty; ty zakokhuyeshsya v n'oho. Meni ne potribno buty z toboyu pov"yazanym mental'no, shchob pobachyty tse.) / Don't deny it; you are falling in love with him. I don't need to be connected to you mentally to see that."

"Хтось ось-ось розірве її дупу, якщо вона не замовкне! (Khtos' os'-os' rozirve yiyi dupu, yakshcho vona ne zamovkne!) / Someone is about to get her ass busted if she does not shut up!"

Since they were great friends, they always teased each other over nearly everything. Trust me, no one realized what Sophia was feeling regarding Zak Harris.

Ms. Miyu said, "Before we go any further, I think it is important to understand some basic principles. In Buddhism, they have Four

Noble Truths. 1. Duḥkha. Since this is a sociology class and not a religious one, I will describe it this way — the illusion of oneself. Think of the word, egoistic; it is the falsehood of ego. An example of it would be arrogance. That is the suffering Buddhism is referring to if I understand right. Maybe someone could research this aspect. Don't worry, Buddhism is not a religion. You will not be digging into religious matters. The other three are a bit to go into, and I don't want to take up your time on it, but it is something to realize and may understand how the hive mind works." She paused, "why I mentioned this is easy. We are no better or worse once we connect to this hive network. We can improve ourselves with or without it."

Zak asked, "Since there is no perfect world, I have to guess, there are arrogant individuals living in this hive system?"

"There is no guess about it, but you are correct. No one has stopped being an individual. We share our minds with everyone else in ways that really can't be explained. Sophia had a great idea — having you link up on a temporal basis. How long you stay within is completely up to you?"

A bit nervous in asking, but he did so anyhow, "How many have done this temporarily?"

Sophia answered, "I think you have the wrong mindset because this is new to you. It is why I only suggested you temporarily connect. How many, right now, does not matter. How many have disconnected and never reconnected is not known either. Before I connected, I was told, like everyone else, we have choices in our lives. Privacy of all is protected completely. Know this, Mr. Harris, your mind will never be an open book to the hive completely. What you do share to the hive may never be understood or realized until others can understand you on just about every level."

Since that is all that can be said on the matter, Ms. Miyu continued on the project. "As for this questionnaire, we got a name, gender, age, and national origin. Any other ideas?" She paused, "I want to point out that the name itself will be kept confidential when the information is tallied."

Someone said, "What about education status?"

She replied, "Great idea." She typed it in.

The same student asked, "Would it be rude to ask about connection status?"

"No, it would not." She typed that suggestion in.

A student by the name of Grace Collins asked, "Since you have talked a little about philosophical aspects of humans connected to the hive, how important is it to this questionnaire?"

"Grace, that is the ultimate question. It could be the best one to ask. What should be asked is the question. Does anyone have any ideas?"

Sophia said, "What about what they know of collective consciousness itself?"

Ms. Miyu was impressed. "Sophia, I think you know more about the question you gave your father yesterday than you may realize. From the look of everyone, not many can answer this. If I am right, I think you do, but that does not mean you can't learn more. There is one absolute thing about life, you will never know enough. 'A frog in a well knows nothing of the sea.' With this class, I know everyone will learn a great deal. Welcome to Sociology." She paused, "as you all will learn more, we can add more to this questionnaire. What we have is a lot more than you may realize."

Since the class time was about over, the students gathered their belongings and took off.

****

Shortly after the school was done for the day, Zak met up with Sophia outside in the parking lot waiting for her mother to pick her up. He said, "I want to thank you for offering me a chance to connect to the hive temporarily. I did not realize, so many did that."

She smiled warmly, "I am glad to have helped." By the looks of him, she realized he had done some research. She asked, "I see you have learned a great deal since, yes?"

"Yes, I have. You are right, nothing on how many have tried this and departed."

"Even if you found anyone to discuss this further, this is completely up to you, Zak. No one can live your life for you. Being connected to the hive does not hinder or help you to be a better person. You may learn new things, but that is life." She paused, "I am learning as you are."

"OH? I thought you knew a great deal."

"Not even close." She paused, "the reason Ms. Miyu started this project had to do with my ignorance of why there are people not connected to the hive. Since today's class and learning from you a lot more than I could hope..."

In a shocked tone, "Little olé me?"

With seriousness, "Yes, you. The more I am learning, the more I realized I was a bit biased toward those who have not connected. I am not telling you this for redemption, but you have interested me a great deal. I did not offer you this temporary connection to force you into anything either." She paused, "what I am trying to say, is I think you allowed me to see something in myself. Wherever you go with this Zak, I will do all I can to help you. The final result is for you to decide."

He gave a warm smile of his own, "Thanks."

Suddenly Sophia got a hive message from her mother, "I will be late, dear. You can meet me with Zak at the nearby malt shop. I don't know how long you will wait. I have talked to his parents, and we can take him home then. At least talk to him about at least you two connecting. It will help both of you with this class project."

She replied, "Since we don't use cell phone communication, yes, that would be a better choice. I would expect..."

"Don't worry about that. You are overthinking again, baby. See you two then."

She told him about the conversation she had with her mother.

"Yes, my parents are connected to the hive. I am not upset with your mother knowing, but how did she know this?"

Sophia smiled, "She is a librarian, and she knows nearly everyone. As far as knowing about you with me, that is easy — I am starting to have a stronger interest in you since class."

"Same here, Sophia. Same here." He thought for a moment, "how will we communicate? We don't use cell phones either."

"I can give you Nanobots, so we can only communicate with each other. Never know, it may help you decide and learn more about connecting to the hive as a whole that textbooks would not have a clue."

He smiled with more interest than fear, "That would be cool! How? My parents have not done this with me or my sister. She had not yet connected."

Sophia held out her hand with her palm facing up. Seconds later, a small cylinder object appeared in her hand.

Zak asked, "What is that?"

"That is how I will give you those Nanobots." She smiled, "ready?"

"Sure."

"If you would expose the right side of your head more."

After leaning his head in the right way, she pressed the object in her hand for a few seconds.

He asked inquisitively, "That is it?"

She answered him after a few seconds more, "If you hear me in your head, yes."

"OH MY, GOODNESS!" After calming down a bit, "yes, I hear you. WOW!"

"There is more you can do when you are connected to the hive mind — even temporarily. What my mom suggested is a basic communication ability. Our conversation is between us, only."

"I am getting more excited, but what little I have learned earlier, I decided to take this slow."

"Believe it or not my dear Zak, that is what we all have done."

As they were talking more in their minds, they continued walking to the nearest small restaurant — what Sophia's mother called a malt shop. She ordered two strawberry floats once they reached the counter.

After they sat down, Sophia whispered, "We can flex your muscles as it were on how we were communicating, later. As we wait, you can share what you have learned so far."

"Can you read my thoughts?"

She gave a gentle smile, "If I could or not, that is not important. I mean, the hive mind is more than having our minds connected. It is what humanity has been doing since the Neanderthals. Even in the 23rd century, Europeans and the United States still have around one to six percent Neanderthal genes in our bodies. Since then, we human beings have been socially connected throughout existence.

The new elements of our technologies have only deepened that desire — collective consciousness."

With more interest, "You mean the tribes of ancient times to the growing population of cities?"

"Exactly! Once you learn more about culture from ancient times to this very day, you may learn more about yourself as you learn about this. I have done." She paused, "at times, I am realizing I have learned nothing if I am this biased."

"Trust me, Sophia, you are not that way, or you would not have helped me. There is no reason to feel guilty about your question. Believe it or not, being on the outside of the hive, I may be biased. We all have questions about the people on the other side of the hill. Believe it or not, that is not biased. It is normal. You want to know about people that are different." He thought to throw what she said back at her, "Why not learn more about yourself as you lead this class project."

She gave a big smile, "You have a great idea."

For some reason, and it may be because of her strong emotions, he could almost read her mind. He said through those Nanobots, "I love you too, Sophia. As you will be for me, I will be there for you."

Sophia could read his thoughts and not just because of their private communication connection. She is falling in love with him more and more. If anything, love is more powerful than the Nanobots that recently entered him that came from her. It is why they can communicate in the way they have, and they will continue to do so.

4

⸺ ❖ ⸺

CHAPTER 3

The next morning, Sophia felt a little nauseated after she woke up. She also felt cramps in her stomach. Since she knew she was in good health, she concentrated on Zak. Realizing it was him, she said in her mind, "Are you okay?"

It took a moment, "Yes, I think so. I hope I am not being too forward, but I had a bout of diarrhea."

"You were not, Zak." She paused, "are you lactose intolerant?"

"I don't think so."

"How I just felt after I woke up..."

"OH MY! You could feel that? We may need to disconnect..."

"I am fine. Yes, I can feel what you are going through, but it was not what I put in you yesterday. We have a stronger bond. There is no reason to get scared over it." She paused, "how I felt from you was just that. I am not sick or the like. How you are feeling right now, I think you are lactose intolerant."

"If I am, that is the first time I have known it."

She closed her eyes, and concentrated, "How do you feel now?"

"OH my! Did you do that?"

She gave him a warm feeling. "Yes, I did. Please tell your parents what I did for you and what you ate after school. How I am feeling about you now, you should be able to go to your classes. If there is anything I am not seeing in you, your parents should help you deal with it. See you soon."

"I will do as you ask, Sophia. How I am feeling, I should be fine, and feeling much better."

"Great! Let me know if you need anything before we meet up in school."

After she got undressed and showered, she went to eat breakfast.

Her mom asked, "How is Zak this morning?"

She told her about what just occurred.

"I had a feeling you would have felt what he went through."

"So that is why you suggested we should connect?"

"One reason, yes. I could feel how much you were in love with him before Yeva teased you about it."

She smiled, "We both are, and I think it is why I felt what he was going through earlier. I even helped him feel a little better."

"It was not because of those Nanobots. They are not medically inclined. What you did was a simple suggestion. You got him to focus on your love for him."

After taking a bite of her breakfast, "I won't bust Yeva's ass as hard, but she is a goofball."

Pippa laughed, "Yes, she is. She was teasing you because you needed to focus on the class at hand. We talked about it."

As Nikolas was coming to the table to eat himself, he said, "Why not invite him here one day? I will help him more about the hive, and you two need to spend time together more."

Seeing her daughter getting embarrassed more than nervous, her mother said, "This isn't your first date, sweetie. Just be yourself. If he is falling in genuine love with you, then he will not expect you to be anything but you."

She shared all they did in her sociology class, yesterday.

Pippa said, "You should be in charge. This project is more for you, but because most may not realize that humanity has been collecting itself over the centuries, then they will learn from you far more than from what Noda Miyu could teach them."

After eating a few more bites, "What she told me. I was the one to suggest having Zak temporarily connected. She did not do that to me. I was a bit shocked..."

Zak appeared so all of them could see him. "I was not shocked at all or disturbed by it."

In alarm, Sophia asked, "How can you present yourself to us all? I see that Bampás and mom can see you. HOW?"

"With the help from mom, I can do this. When it is time for me to temporarily or permanently connect to the hive, I want you to do so — especially after you felt what I went through earlier. This hive mind did not do this — you did. I am grateful for it."

Sophia smiled warmly. "What can we do for you, my love?" She was a bit taken aback, she expressed her true love so openly.

"I love you too, Sophia." He paused, "what I faced earlier was not because of drinking that strawberry float."

"What is wrong?"

"It may be nothing, but mom wants me to be checked by a doctor, so I will let you know the results."

With her eyes opened, "I don't see any other disturbances in you."

"Mom did not either. She took my temperature, and I had a bit of a fever. No, it was not because of the Nanobots."

"I hope it is nothing serious. Those bots in your head are not medical inclined, but they can monitor your vitals."

Pippa said, "My daughter, you are not medically inclined either. Zak, for you to show yourself and talk to us all here, I think you will turn out fine, but I recall I did something similar with Sophia when she was younger."

"If you don't show up in class today, I will let Ms. Miyu know about it."

"Mom said, she got that taken care of. Please take notes for me if I don't."

She smiled warmly again, "I will, love. Hear from you soon."

He vanished.

Her father said, "He will be alright."

****

During lunchtime and at the cafeteria, Sophia thought to check on Zak.

After Somova and Yeva sat in one of the chairs at the table, Somova asked, "How is he doing?"

She looked at her and answered, "I think he is sleeping. It is nothing serious."

Yeva said, "Because he had the same symptoms of the olé stomach flu, does not mean it is that."

"I am sure I would have gotten word if it was that serious — like the flu or not."

Yeva smiled, "He will be fine." She paused, "sorry for overly teasing you yesterday."

She smiled, "It is one of your specialties, girlfriend."

"How are you feeling?"

She realized what she meant. She answered, "I am fine. Falling in love with him so suddenly and having him hit by an illness took me off guard."

Somova replied, "What you shared with us, I think he would have talked to you already if it was dire. He loves you just as much."

Through the hive, Zak's mother, Kiara, said, "I hope I am not interrupting anything."

"No, you are not. I am eating lunch with my two girlfriends. How is Zak doing?"

She gave a pleasant feeling and said, "He is doing fine. It was not the stomach flu I was concerned about. The fever was because he is lactose intolerant."

"OH MY. I was the one..."

"It is fine. He just got a mild case."

She sighed inwardly. She recalled he did not recall he was intolerant to dairy products. "If he told me that he did not realize his condition, then he must have been hit by this since he was a baby, yes?"

"Yes, he would not recall that. The doctor said it was not because of that, but I don't believe it."

A bit embarrassed, "I think it is stress." She told her about the class project and about putting the Nanobots in him to just mind-link with him. "I hope I did nothing wrong."

"You did not. He told me about that. That is why we are talking this way." She paused and continued, "he has been very nervous about connecting to the hive. I think he would have been worse if it was not for you, Sophia. Thank you."

"I will make sure he shares his concerns with me. If he does not, then this connection can turn on him."

"I only contacted you to let you know he is okay. I sent messages to all his instructors. You finish eating and don't let this upset you too much."

"Knowing what is going on is helping me relax. I will check on him in a few hours if he does not contact me first."

After the conversation, she told her two friends what had occurred.

****

Once again, she was early in the classroom. Ms. Miyu smiled, "I know you and Zak are connected. I see you are not too upset, so I take it, he is fine?"

"Yes, Kiara talked to me, through the hive, earlier. It seems he was just stressed out from taking the plunge."

She smiled again, "That was what she told me this morning. How are you dealing with it?"

"I wondered if my suggestion was too soon, yes?"

"If it was or not, that is not the point. Zak would have told you to slow down or the like already. From what I gather from Kiara, he has a great love for you. Stop punishing yourself. It will not help him or you."

"OH MY! That is right, he can read my thoughts — especially these strong ones."

"I now know you both will turn out good. Something the two of you were not expecting. Both his mother and I believe if it was not for you to suggest the temporary connection to the hive by adding the Nanobots to have your private conversations, he could have been worse. If anything, Sophia, you turned him in the right direction and put him on track. It was his excess worrying or whatever that was interrupted."

"You mean a person can get sick after he has turned into the light?"

"Most definitely." She paused, "it was not that within itself, but the divorcement, as it were, from his bad decisions of the fears he created about our hive mind network. It has nothing to do with you, this hive-mind technology, or anything else. It was the mental state he was building up. When you helped him let go of that, he felt the weight of it all hit him all too fast on his psyche. When you two connect with the Nanobots or in person, you two will share more of that genuine love. Hold on to that."

She replied, "□□□□□□ (Arigatō.) / Thank you" before sitting at a desk.

****

After everyone else got seated, Ms. Miyu asked, "What have you all gathered so far with this project?"

A fifteen-year-old student by the name of Abigail Perry said, "Since you talked about Buddhism, I thought to dig into what Hinduism had to say on the subject." She pulled out what she wrote and continued, "I learned there are five principles: 1. God Exists, 2. All Human Beings Are Divine. 3. Unity of Existence, 4. Religious Harmony, and 5. Knowledge of 3 Gs." She paused, "doing more research, I believe numbers 2 through 4 might apply to this project. They appear, to me, they are like our hive mind collectives."

She was impressed and showed it. "Fabulous, Ms. Perry. Please hold onto that and keep learning." She paused, "know this class, no one religion teaches us about life, but it all has its basic wonders and damnation. What I mean is through corruption, any institution has been manipulated for power lust for one reason or the other. Their teachings on the other hand — what is called doctrine — teach a similar approach to these five principles. There are other walks of life we should investigate. Why I mentioned Buddhism, it was never classified as a religion, but through the same corruption of certain leaders, they too have to face such fate."

A student asked, "Can we trust their sources?"

"Good question. It is why no instructor will ask you to use just one source. Even if it is a good one, it may be a bit weak to hold up your claims. Before you ask it, yes, there is a lot of misinformation. That is a sad aspect of life. It had started when the first time someone lied. If you learn anything in my sociology class, please know this. Some people will still con or manipulate anyone. Even under our hive mind collective consciousness, there will be criminals who harm others. Friedrich Nietzsche said, 'The surest way to corrupt a youth is to instruct him to hold in higher esteem those who think alike than those who think differently.' Our hive mind system does not violate this principle. Instead, it enhances it by allowing all who are connected to be an individual rather than a controlled one-minded drone."

Hearing that through Sophia, Zak had a great deal of weight leave him. Sophia said on his behalf, "Zak told me to say, 'that is what I needed to hear. It has been worrying me for several years now. I know now, it is why I got sick today. A jaunt for nothing, I realize now, but I am very relieved to hear this from you.'"

Ms. Miyu smiled, "I will allow Sophia to share with you more on this very thing. I am surprised after looking into everyone's eyes as I was stating this quote, no one knew of it or heard of Nietzsche. There is another thing you can learn. Under any modern technology, no one can learn everything. Socrates once said, 'The only true wisdom consists in knowing that you know nothing.' If the hive gives us anything, it is ignorance. We all have to learn on our merit."

Sophia said, "She is right, my love. You do not have to worry about this anymore. I will be there for you anytime. This is one of several hurdles before you will be ready to take the plunge in connecting to the hive mind temporarily. I will be there for you all the way."

"I know, my lovely Sophia. Thank you."

Sophia finally nodded to the instructor that everything was fine.

The rest of the class went on with other things about sociology. Ms. Miyu was impressed, this one student gathered that much on the project so quickly. Since this was a project-based one, she realized they need to do all the work. She will be there to guide them, and it seemed she gave the best advice.

****

As expected, Sophia went to meet up with Zak at his home. Both Kiara and Zak's father [Patrick] were expecting her to come to their home after school. Pippa dropped her off since she wasn't old enough to drive yet. After the warm welcome, she met up with Zak in the living room.

He said, "Thanks for dropping by."

After she had a seat, she said, "Talk to me. I felt more in your head."

He explained what he recently read. "It was some old data, but it was the first book I saw."

"If I am reading your facial expressions right, I think it was one of the books I read not too long ago. If I were not already connected, I too would be as concerned and confused. I am sure your confusion lies within seeing tons of people are fine and dandy while wondering how strong of an influence the writer got you hooked on."

"It wasn't a direct dystopian style, but the writer nearly got me to think of something worse."

"How do you feel now about it?"

"After hearing Ms. Miyu quoting Nietzsche, I believe I shook that horrible influence out of my head." He paused, "this has allowed me to be timid, but I want to know all I can. The right information would not hurt, either."

She smiled, "No kidding." She paused, "I talked to mom as she drove me here after today's classes. Tomorrow, mom should have some right materials for you to read." She paused once more, "you are right to get upset. Hell! Anyone would have. This is something new to you."

"I know one thing, I am confident in." He waited to dramatize the moment, "I know I love you and trust what you do share with me."

Patrick suggested, "Why not talk to the school's librarian to get rid of that book that has false implications in it? By now, they have gotten rid of a lot of such books, but no one is perfect. This one eluded them."

With her eyes opened, she felt deep in Zak's psyche. "I don't feel any negative influence on you."

He stated, "If I did, I assure you, I would have shared it with you."

"That is not what I meant, love. Why I probed your deep thoughts, I recall I was bothered by something, and it took a dear friend to help me see that in me."

Kiara said, "Yes, baby. I, too, was concerned about this."

Sophia smiled, "Since it was something you read recently, its influences could not go that deep, but I wanted to make sure."

"Thanks for doing that, my love. After I puked coming home, I felt better."

A bit disturbed by it. "I thought I felt that in you. I want to do that the moment after."

"Wow! They are strong Nanobots for you to feel that in me."

Kiara replied, "It has nothing to do with technology, Zak. It has to do with her love for you. She may be monitoring you too much, but her heart is in the right place."

For the first time, they kissed each other.

Zak said, "WOW! That was some kiss."

"You will always get the best from me."

They ended up kissing once more but more passionately.

****

After spending more romantic time, Sophia shared with her lover about the class and the project. She said, "Let me remind you that a civilization 'is a complex society that is characterized by urban development, social stratification, a form of government, and symbolic systems of communication beyond natural spoken language' (https://en.wikipedia.org/wiki/Civilization). A hive mind system is no different. As you are aware, we first connect to our local network. It is connected dynamically to the main city. I think we have a few hubs. It has been a while since I was told this. Bigger the city, the more local hubs. Our city is connected or adjacent to all the cities in the State. Like a gateway to the Internet, the State hive is dynamically connected to the other States."

He asked, "Connected dynamically, you mean they flow as if they are one big hive?"

"In a way, yes. It is more to it than that. It is why this system and not the main central world hive? That is easy. It allows growth and individuality to prosper. Forget the old dystopian stories, movies, and television shows. That's all fantasy... if not outright stupid. I would not be here with you if I was a mindless drone."

"That is great to know."

She smiled lovingly, "I doubt hardly anyone would be connected, or the damn thing would exist if humans were turned into nothingness. What would the purpose be in creating something so inspirational if it would destroy who we were? Instead, we can share more of who we are as individuals, a culture, and all that makes us humans more than we had done with the Internet that was given to us in the early 1990s. It is why it evolved so powerfully because humanity wanted to continue with this collective consciousness."

Overwhelmed, "I will be damned! So, this hive mind network is the simple evolution of this Internet and the thriving collective of humanity that started with the Neanderthals?"

She gave him a big warm smile, "That is it exactly. It has evolved far more than expected since the first stages. Each one of us can be ourselves while sharing ourselves, giving support, and learning beyond anything known to humanity throughout Earth's history."

5

CHAPTER 4

Before all the students at Correlative Attentive High School realized it, it was Saturday. People today may think that is an odd name for a school's name. If only the people of the 21st century were connected to a hive mind network, they may think differently. As I stated, the year 2200 may not be fully understood because the mental framework is so different. I will let you study this on your own. Learning something important, like time was never linear, takes time. Because these people worldwide are mentally connected, it does not mean they know everything. Learning is an individual process because it takes experience to apply knowledge. In Greek, GNOSIS and EPIGNOSIS are similar words upfront, but in reality, they are two unique words.

GNOSIS means to know. It is like putting food on a plate. We can see what is on the plate, but it is not understood knowledge. EPIGNOSIS is metabolized and processed information. As you eat — a bite at a time, the food on the plate — knowledge learned is understood because you have experienced it. As you learn more about life, that experience is compounded through many process-es. Knowledge in a book sitting on a bookshelf does nothing for you until experiences — your experiences — are applied. That is why in a hive mind network, no one's mental state is in jeopardy, lost, or absorbed in some central storage somewhere. How much can the human brain store? More than you can imagine.

"The human brain's memory capacity in the average adult can store trillions of bytes of information... according to a 2010 article in Scientific American, the memory capacity of the human brain was reported to have the equivalent of 2.5 petabytes of memory capacity. As a number, a "petabyte" means 1024 terabytes or a million gigabytes, so the average adult human brain can store the equivalent of 2.5 million gigabytes digital memory. (https://www.cnsnevada.com/what-is-the-memory-capacity-of-a-human-brain/)"

It is not hard to come to realize — all the minds connected to the hive are not brainless puppets. They are not all Albert Einstein, either, or the same as they were before they completely and freely chose to connect and share their thoughts, experiences, and way of life with everyone else. They learned more on their own like everyone else through the educational systems, reading, and applying it all to their personal lives. It is no different from joining a group, having friends, being a part of your neighborhood, and all the rest we do — if we realize it or not. As you grow and evolve with everyone else, you start to become a part of society. Collective consciousness simply means, "the set of shared beliefs, ideas, and moral attitudes which operate as a unifying force within a society."

Everyone in many societies is not controlled by the leader of said group. Sometimes corruption makes people into drones, but those individuals choose to do so. Like the Devil card in a tarot deck, the devil knows his slaves can leave anytime, but for some crazy reason, they choose to be slaves. We all have choices in life, no matter what our status may be. Anyone can manipulate themselves and interlock themselves in a hole so deep — they may never get out of it, but they chose to make the wrong choices.

What destroys society in any growth is ignorance. Many during the preindustrial age feared the unknown. They thought the machines would take their jobs. We are starting to fear artificial intelligence will do the same today. If the old thing is gone and passed away, why fear the old? Why not embrace the new? I don't know many who fear knowledge — just keep learning.

Right now, artificial intelligence has the mind of a cockroach. Maybe in five or seven years, it may have the intelligence of a lab rat. Only Hollywood, television shows, and novels tell us all today's technology will one day take over humanity. This is not reality at all. I recalled people feared the first personal computers in the 80s. Believe it or not, humans will always find something to fear even when it is a complete illusion.

****

By communicating through the hive mind, Sophia got all the students of the sociology class to gather at the State Park that afternoon. When everyone arrived, Sophia said, "Thank you all for coming. We need to organize this class project. As we all got from Ms. Miyu's mind, we are all responsible for this project. She will guide us when it is required... nothing more. By having us build on what we all will be doing, we can start this project now rather than later."

Abigail Perry asked, "How detailed do you want to go with this?"

She looked at Zak and back at her, "As you know by now, I was the one to ask my father why are people not connected to our hive network." Abigail nodded, "the more research we can do, the better

— both the ones that have not been connected and the ones who have already. If it was just me, I could have done all this myself."

Zak said, "Nonsense! I now realize how intelligent you are, my love, but you need a team to help you. I want to know because I am one of the individuals that have not yet connected."

Everyone there vowed to guide and support him in this important task.

"Thanks, guys. It is the unlearning of all the misguided information I have learned over the years."

Sophia smiled, "Since that book has been removed from the school's library, at least that one will not trouble you anymore. I told the librarian, I would not mind burning the damn thing."

Abigail said, "Since I dug up the information I shared with the class the other day, I will focus on the philosophical if not the religious aspect."

Sophia said, "Great idea. I think we need to concentrate on several aspects." She picked up the paper that had the list. "Zak had already been given the archaeology or historical aspect. Since we are doing this in our sociology class, I will take up that responsibility; I mean the sociology part. That leaves two more I would like to focus on — anthropology and interpersonal Intelligence. Since we have 25 students here — which is the whole class, we should work in groups. Abigail and Zak can be the group leader of their subprojects. Who wants to be the leader of the other two?"

Since Jorgie Watts loves to learn and study linguistics, she thought to take the plunge of being the leader of the anthropology aspect of the project.

Cooper Marsh, a science buff, asked, "What does anthropology have to do with this project?"

Sophia said, "That is an interesting question. Here is my answer. As we all know, the Europeans and the American descendants have around 1 to 6 percent Neanderthal genome in our bodies. That has to mean they socialized with the Cro-Magnons, or we would not have any genetic connection with them. This is a sociological assignment, so they had a part in some form of collective consciousness. How little social intelligence they had, it must have been for pure survival rather than some early-man social understanding as we know it."

Abigail asked, "What does Ms. Miyu want us to find?"

"All we can, but it will be in an unusual manner. My mom said she will help us find what we need to know at the library. We were discussing this very thing. What I understood from her — we will need to discover how intelligent they were, what they may have learned from the Cro-Magnon humans, and do our best to put the necessary puzzle pieces and come out with the best answers."

Cooper decided to be the leader of the interpersonal Intelligence group.

Sophia continued, "Great! We have our groups. Now for the fun part — gathering the information. Remember, my mother, runs our public library. She told me she is ready to help all of you, but she will not do the project for us."

Jorgie said, "In knowing about the fun of doing science research and knowing about how a library is run, it would be wrong for her or anyone else to gather the research. Learning is more than the destination. It is always the journey. That is why all twenty-five of us will learn a great deal more than we can dream possible."

As they were discussing this project, Sophia caught an interest in a group at a good distance from them. It was after the class left, she decided to learn more.

Zak said, "If I understand right, they are against this hive mind."

Sophia said, "OH. They don't look hostile."

"No, they don't. I still don't see how meeting them will do any good."

"It may not, but showing some hospitality, may do something." She paused, "besides, not much they can do about stopping anyone or anything."

Before Zak could say more, she walked closer to one of them. He followed her but casually.

"Hi, there. I am Sophia Vitaloti. My sociology class was gathering earlier on a high school project. Seeing you all here, I was interested in saying hello."

A young adult female replied without smiling, "We have gathered ourselves in our project."

Showing a polite interest, "Cool."

"I don't think you would enjoy what we are doing."

"Please, let me be the judge of that. I promise I will not bite."

"Okay... you asked for it. We are against this hive mind system."

"What a coincidence, our class project is about it. It is gathering the history of collective consciousness and how it developed into what you are calling — a hive mind."

She looked confused and sounded a bit harsh, "Are you telling me, humanity wanted to be connected like this? That is hard for me to swallow."

Sophia smiled, "I think I am going to like you." She paused, "this project came from a question I asked my Bampás... well what I call my father, anyhow. It is a Greek word that means father."

She had a hunch she was already connected to this hive network, but it seems her question may be something that could interest her. "Are you saying you are against this system?"

"Not exactly, and I was told I was not being biased about it." She sighed, "I asked, why are some people not already connected?"

The young woman smiled, "I may like you, too." She paused, "trust me, Sophia, you were not being ugly. Asking such a question may have given me a different point of view on this system you are connected to. If I am right, you are connected, yes?"

"Yes, I have been since the age of nine. I am 17 years old." Having the young woman show nervousness, Sophia said, "as I said, I will not bite." She turned to look at her lover. She said while looking at him, "this is my boyfriend, Zak Harris."

"Hello. My name is Scarlet Knox. It is great to meet you both." It was not until after Sophia looked back at her, she spoke, "it may be me that could be biased or whatever one may call it. My group was talking about how disgusted we are with this network. Some people believe in conspiracies and that all of you are mindless drones or the like. After experiencing you both, I am starting to believe all of you are just as normal as the ones who are not connected."

"Believe it or not, Zak is not yet connected. We do have a private mental connection."

"That is interesting. I did not know it was that easy to do that."

"The process is through advanced Nanotechnologies. It is completely painless to have them enter you or anyone else." Feeling her mother was about to arrive, she said, "why not check out the library? My mother, Pippa Gill Vitaloti, is the head librarian. She will be happy to help you."

"HOLY COW! I love going to that library. She is your mother?"

She gleefully nodded.

When Pippa came closer, she said, "Hello. Don't tell me, you are already a friend of my daughter."

"She does have her charms. It is great to meet you... again."

"Same here, Scarlet." Out of politeness, she did not comment on what she got from her daughter's mind. She realized Ms. Knox had to talk first about it.

"We were discussing that I could learn a great deal about the hive mind system you all are connected to. Yes, I am against it, but I am not hateful about it. Neither are the ones here earlier."

"I will do all I can to help. There is nothing to fear with it. As I told Sophia the other day, if I could not be myself after I was connected, I would not have done so."

"Your daughter told me, this collective consciousness has been around for a long time, and this technology evolved from this. That is the first time I heard about it."

"It is more to it than that but yes. After my daughter's class project is done, you may want to read it... if not take part in it."

Sophia said, "We are slowly building a questionnaire. It may be after we gather and build this project that it can be distributed. We all just started with it this semester. Our meeting here today was to organize it, so we can get it rolling."

"How do we contact each other? I take it, you guys don't use cell phones to talk."

Sophia answered, "That is correct. We can meet here next week or whenever. I am at Correlative Attentive High School during the weekdays."

"I can relay any information to your mother if I need you for anything. I might connect with you as you have with your boyfriend. I take it you can do so with several people in this private network?"

"Oh, yes! Zak is not the first one. It has been years with the others, and I severed our connection when they moved to another country. It was sad for both of us, and I don't know if they are connected to the hive system or not. I have not heard from them since."

Pippa said, "No one will ever force you to connect — with my daughter's private connection or any other."

Sensing they needed to go, Sophia said, "I would love to learn more about you and your point of view. Trust me; it is important to me."

Scarlet smiled, "I will be happy to do that. Thank you for your insights, too."

Pippa, Sophia, and Zak departed.

As they were driving, Zak said, "That went better than expected."

Sophia said, "Yes, it did. I wonder if it was too well? I hope I am getting the wrong vibes, but..."

Pippa said, "You are not. She has shown her strong negativities before. It does not mean she has not improved, but a lot of the books she reads are against our hive system."

"Mom, you mean you can't get rid of those books?"

After stopping at a light, she answered, "If we removed any information against our opinion, we could not learn anything new. We would end up being too stuck up to learn outside our experiences."

Zak said, "I was against this hive network, but I have learned a few new things that have changed my mind before this class project got started. It is why I knew her, and I believe she may have done the same — to an extent. If she is willing to join in our private communication, then that is a good thing."

Pippa said, "That is true, but be careful you two. Lighter the picture, darker the negative."

"Mom, what should we be looking for? I know I was the one to take the plunge in meeting her for the first time, but..."

"Right now, nothing. Let her make the first move. If she is genuine as Zak is professing, then nothing bad will happen. Expect some bitterness from her or the friends she hangs out with."

"I was expecting something before I walked up to her, but at the same time, I felt it was the right thing to do. I still feel that way."

Pippa smiled after making a left turn, "I had to admit, I did not feel you distressed over talking to her."

Zak replied, "Neither did I."

"Mom, how long ago was it when she showed frustration in front of you?"

"It could be nothing, baby, and she was friendly before I came up to you all. I could be wrong, and I hope I am."

"We did not talk much, I admit, but I did not feel any harshness from her. I guess when I told her about humanity having been collecting themselves nearly at the very beginning, she seemed more enthusiastic over it than frustrated."

"That is true."

Zak asked, "Do you have some telepathic abilities? You seem to be very empathetic."

Pippa said, "She has been attuned to others' feelings nearly since she was born."

Sophia continued, "I am not telepathic because of that or being connected to the hive. As mom said, I can understand what others are feeling." She paused, "I am not always right about such matters. I do my best to learn from my mistakes and keep on trusting in my abilities."

Zak said, "It would not surprise me if Scarlet saw that in you."

After turning a right turn, "That my dear Zak could make her dangerous if she still has any bitterness towards others that are connected to the hive."

"Mom, surely all these many years, the fears of this hive-mind system have allowed others to know there are no dangers."

Zak said, "Don't be so sure about that, my love. It was this class project and our private connection that opened my mind up. Ignorance always causes fear even for over a thousand years."

Her mother said, "It is why you are the leader of this project. Most are still ignorant about the history of how humanity has been collecting itself which has created nations all around the globe. Technology can be a cold tool. The only thing that makes it alive and dynamic is the understanding of how we got to where we are today. Tools don't enhance humanity. It is using the right mindset by how we use those tools."

6

— • —

Chapter 5

Not long after dropping Zak at his home and before both Pippa and Sophia drove onto the driveway, she thought she should write a complimentary paper on the project. "At least it will be a guide on how I asked Bampás the other day and why this project is being done in this class. If I don't write this, I may go out of my mind. There is either something I am not admitting or something I need to grasp before I can do my part if not answer my question."

After she arrived in her room, she got ahold of her lover and told him what she had in mind.

"My love. That is a wonderful idea. I suggest writing it without being too concerned with the length, grammar, etc. With my class papers, I end up correcting them all over the place. This one is for you to do. It must come from within yourself."

"I agree." She paused, "you got a good point. I don't think Scarlet had anything to do with it, but she got me to focus more on what I originally asked Bampás."

"If you need anything, please let me know."

"I will do just that. I think I need you to connect with me more than you do."

"Then you are doing the right thing, and you proved your question is not biased."

"Thanks, my love."

She got off her bed and sat at her desk. On her computer, she opened the software to write her essay, complementary paper, or whatever it should be called...

~~~~~

Since the dawn of humanity, we strive to collect ourselves for the better of our existence. There is nothing from the Neanderthals about why they did so with the Cro-Magnons or from those people either. Since they both lived in extremely harsh conditions, we have to conclude that it was for pure survival. Since the early 21st century to the modern era of our existence, I am wondering if the main reason we have this hive-mind network is for our survival.

I believe it is why I asked the question that started this Sociology Class Project — why have a good many of the people of Earth since decades of having this hive system not been connected? Could it be for the same reasons as the huge misinformation that caused the meltdown of American society just because one person did not want to accept he lost the race to the office of the President of the United States of America? If so, this is an old vendetta.

People have told me my question that started this project was not biased. I don't want to stir things up again, but I wonder if the dust of yesteryear has settled. It has been way over a century since that political sham started, but I believe it is still ongoing. How will our way of life be affected in this nation and all the others around the world? There were no alarm bells to warn us of what had occurred. If I know my history, there usually are no warnings. Corruption always starts delicately and ever so slowly. Like putting a
~~~~~

frog in hot boiling water, it will jump out before it is hurt. Otherwise, if he is put in cold water while on an eye of a stove and the heat was turned to the lowest setting, he could boil to death before it could respond to the danger.

How many groups are there congregating to form something against our hive network? If only I could do something... educate people like Scarlet. She appeared to be interested in what little I shared. Will this project be enough? Thinking about it, not many have educated a mass full of people at the time the hive system started. Maybe this project will start doing that to the new generations.

Since I am the leader of this project and not the world or this nation for that matter, I will make sure everyone has this in mind. I wonder if that is why I asked my question to Bampás? I don't know the important things about why we started the hive-mind network in the first place. When I wrote, 'I am wondering if the main reason we have this hive-mind network is for our survival,' I felt something strongly, it was more out of desperation than scientific progress. Even if I learn all I can, would it help change the minds of people who are fighting this system, today?

If it were not for learning about the people who could be gathering to fight how we live today, this class project could easily be created for the future, but the past seems to be holding on just as strongly as it did on January 6, 2021. If I am worrying over phantoms, then the worst-case scenario will never happen. Whatever the future may be, this project must be a beacon to holding humanity together.

~~~~~

Sophia thought to send the very rough draft of this paper to Ms. Noda Miyu. After a short time, she replied...
~~~~~

~~~~~

Ms. Sophia Vitaloti,

I am very impressed with what you wrote. Believe it or not, that is why I immediately wanted this project done by all of you in your class. When I sent all this to the proper school authorities, Principle Lydia Day could not agree with it fast enough.

Please understand that the hatred that was started on January 6, 2021, has never burned out. The racism of the 1950s never did either. Even under our hive-mind network, these types of behaviors have not calmed down. None of us may ever achieve that goal. Please do not feel you have failed by asking this vitally important question to your father. Trust me, Sophia, you have the right mind-set by asking. As you learn more, maybe you can learn the history of our hive-mind system by why it got started in the first place.

Just be the best you can be. Your leadership will have many to follow. Trust me when I say this — every class member has great respect for you... especially what you did at the park earlier today. I can't share what they told me directly — because that is a private matter, but everyone will support you all the way.

Believe it or not, Scarlet Knox wrote to me not too long ago. She told me she researched online about what you shared with her. She wanted me to tell you, she got most of those gathered in the same park to turn 180 degrees around their views against the hive-mind network. How many are against it, she does not know. I have to guess these people are few and scattered. Ms. Knox will do everything she can to make sure everyone learns about our class project. We may have a good many to fill out that questionnaire once it is ready to be distributed.
~~~~~

Hold fast to what you believe and never lose faith in yourself. See you Monday.

Your Enthusiastic Sociology instructor,

Ms. Noda Miyu

~~~~~

Sophia was not fully convinced. She was concerned about the outcome of the past and what may occur.

She often does not get information directly from the hive mind, but then she is only 17 years old. Even though it was in her head, it sounded like an Indian dialect, "If you fail to wage this war of sacred duty, you will abandon your duty and fame only to gain evil."

She replied, "What war? OH! MY!"

"Nonsense child. I just recited the words from the Bhagavad-GÚtÍ. It was from the word from Krishna. There is nothing to fear." Waited for her to calm her mind. The voice continued, "why I shared that with you is simple. You must face your duty not only the question you willfully gave your Bampás but the class project that is given to you. The task at hand is not for you to be responsible for what others have done or will do. Through this class project, deal with what you can control."

She understood the person to whom he spoke. He is one of the gods of the Hindu faith, but she is still troubled by what had expired, "So I was not biased by my question? At times, I feel I was."

"Never be ashamed of your responsibilities because shame is worse than death. Your heart guided you to ask this question. There is no shame in asking something from your own heart."

"Is my heart pure?"

"No one is perfect, child. Yes, you are 17 years old, but you are still a child who is inexperienced and a child to Krishna." The voice
~~~~~

paused and continued, "be intent on action, not the fruits of action; avoid attraction to the fruits and attachment to inaction. Perform actions, firm in discipline, relinquishing attachment; be impartial to failure and success. This equanimity is called discipline."

Sophia thought for a moment. "You are right, I am afraid to fail. All of a sudden I felt the responsibility of guiding the masses that I do not know into the light of the truth of our hive-mind system."

"It is highly possible Krishna gave you this, but it should not be a burden as you are fearing. Know this child, without discipline, there is no understanding or inner power. Without that, there is no peace. If you continue to be ensnared by your emotions, you have no joy in your heart."

"Are you saying, I should not be concerned about..."

"What is your duty? Is it to be a politician? A hive-mind police officer? What is given to you has everything to do with your question — why? The details do not matter. Yes, you asked, 'why are there people not connected to the hive-mind as you and I are now?'"

"I was upset that these individuals are somehow disturbed by it as if they needed the right information."

"What you said, child, came from you. That means you need to focus on this project. No one will think you are biased against them. They will know you cared enough to take the time in your life to give them what they need to know. As your instructor told you, Scarlet Knox contacted her in a positive light. She did this because of your duty to your question."

She had shown understanding.

"Karma yoga is the discipline of action. Jnana yoga is the discipline of knowledge. Bakhti yoga is the discipline of devotion. If you use these three in your duty, you will succeed. Krishna said,

'All beings find their support in me, whereas I do not depend on them at all.' Everything in life evolves in the cosmic whole of life. It doesn't matter if one is connected to the hive mind or not. If you can learn anything from me, child, it is the journey that is more important than the destination or the why. Your duty and mine are to pay attention to the whole of life. Never just the good, bad, or ugly. Those things are temporal and soon will perish."

Sophia opened her eyes. She smiled, "Hi mom. I thought I felt your presence."

"Yes, baby, I was there to support you. He was right; this is your duty. I, for one, have complete faith in you." Before she had the chance, "stop right there. Instead of overthinking this, apply what that Indian gave you. It is more than you may realize. Give it time."

"For now, I will. Not much I can do about it at the moment."

Through another hive-mind communication, Yeva said excitedly, "Ms. Miyu allowed us all to read that project's complementary paper. GREAT girlfriend!"

"It is the first draft. It will need polishing."

"You're kidding! You mean, you just wrote it on the fly?!"

"Yes, I did. Zak told me to write it from my heart."

"OH, MY GOD! You are a great writer, sweetie."

"From what I got from a Hindu, from India earlier, this is my duty to have this project completed."

"Zak did the right thing, and if this Hindu monk or whoever got from your mind what you wrote, girlfriend, you will never be alone with this. Yes, this is your duty, but after every student has read this paper of yours, they will make you shine."

"You know I am not interested in that. I just want everyone to have the opportunity to learn everything. Zak is in charge of the history aspect, but searching for the very beginning of our hive-mind network will not be easy. I don't know any of it."

Pippa said, "Believe it or not, my daughter, that information is in the library. When Zak and his team come by, I will help them find all he needs to know."

7

— ● —

Chapter 6

It is Monday once again, and every student is back in school. Before they allowed Ms. Miyu to start the class... they all wanted to give their support to Sophia.

Somova said, "I think I speak for the whole class after we all discussed this completely." She paused to dramatize the moment and continued, "Sophia's document complementing the class project should stay the same." The class cheered.

Since Sophia was already standing in front of the whole class, she wanted to cry. She commented, "You all are nuts... but thanks. That is not a paper by any means an essay or anything professional. I wrote it... come to think about it, I don't know why I wrote it at all. I felt like I had to do so, and never thought it would be accepted as part of this class project."

Ms. Miyu said, "Trust me, Sophia, I would not have shared it with every student here, if I did not think it was important. It is one of the best papers I have read. What you wrote was not an essay or an abstract of any kind. When this project is online for all to read..."

Sophia gave an alarming look, "WHAT?!"

"None of that, Ms. Vitaloti!" When she used that tone of voice, it meant she was serious.

"I apologize for my outburst..."

Yeva said, "Don't worry, it is about time to bust her ass anyhow. It is that time of day she usually does."

She gave her that look she does every time she said something like that. "Who will be the one to give it to me, Ms. Fesenko?" She giggled.

She giggled back, "It is a surprise, girly."

Zak said, "I gave you a suggestion to write this from your heart. It was you that wrote it."

Jorgie Watts said, "I don't want her to get that whooping. It is because of that character that allowed her to write that paper we all read."

Ms. Miyu continued, "Ms. Vitaloti, I have also sent that paper to Principle Lydia Day. She wanted it to be used for this project, but she wanted everything to be presented online — once it is completed." She paused to dramatize the moment, "After Scarlet Knox read it, she will fund the means to have it online in all its glory."

Sophia immediately covers her face and starts to tear up."

Yeva said, "We love you, girl."

The entire class cheered loudly.

In her mind that she only heard... Zak said, "I am ready."

More tears of joy ran down her face. He came up to her to give her an endearment hug.

After a short hug and a few more tears going down her face, she asked, "How long do you want to stay connected to the hive."

Yeva suggested, "Until she gets the surname of Harris."

More tears of joy ran down her face. With a crying voice, "I would love that."

He said, "So would I, Ms. Sophia Vitaloti."

She gave a warm loving smile. She said, "I will set it for five years." After he nodded for his approval, she placed her right palm out, and another small cylinder appeared.

He moved his head just right and Sophia did as she had done before.

It was not Yeva that spoke next. It was the same Hindu monk that all in the class heard, "Welcome, Zak Harris. She will guide you in the love she has in her heart for you and everyone in the class. The Veda says, 'Service is proof of real love. Service means the sacrifice of work and sacrifice of the fruit of work. The mother serves her child by the sacrifice of work like giving a bath, dressing etc., for years together continuously. The father serves the child by the sacrifice of the fruit of his entire hard work. It is a clear practical point that the proof of real love is the only service. If you serve your family, you love your family. If you serve the entire world, you love the creation, If you serve God, you love God and this is only devotion.' Her devotion will be the beacon for the whole world regarding this project."

Zak replied, "She has already had and before this project got started."

"Ms. Noda Miyu, Our sangha is willing to help fund this online project here in India if not all over the world. This growing generation has a lot to learn about how the hive-mind system got started. I can't think of a better way to teach them."

She replied, "I completely agree. When I heard her talking to her Bampás, I had to set this project now — for this semester. It appeared I did the right thing. Everything she has done so far has blossomed into wonders beyond my imagination. This is her duty and devotion."

Zak said, "If it were not for her, I would not be connected to the hive-mind even temporarily as it may be. This moment to me is a lifetime — my life... NO! Our lifetime."

They immediately kissed each other passionately. Everyone cheered.

"Love you, Sophia."

"I love you, too."

After their semi-private romantic moment, Zak looked at everyone and said, "Well, now you all can help me as you claimed the other day."

Ms. Miyu said, "We all will, but as you said, 'it will be your life with Sophia.' In that, you are permanently connected to the hive-mind network. WELCOME!"

Everyone cheered — including Sophia.

After he sat down, he said, "This mind communication with all of you is not as bad as I thought."

Sophia said, "It is fear that makes things harder than it is in life. I now realize it is why I asked Bampás that question. I realized more could join this hive-mind once they let go of their fears." She paused, "I also realize, they have a choice. It appears that a good many still refuse to not join us all while being socially intelligent as we all are here."

Ms. Miyu said, "That is why we are doing this project. You, students, will do most of it, true enough, but I have my part. This is your time in life. My generation may have started this hive-mind project — as we all know it today, but you all will have to take up this moment and the future. How things will turn out is completely in your hands. That may sound scary, but it doesn't have to be. It is completely up to you."

****

Humanity has been around for seven million years — from the Sahelanthropus to us today, modern humans. Through those millions of years, many species of humans have grown slowly in intelligence. Tools throughout the Americas have left proof of tools that could not have been made and used. The remarkable aspect of early mankind is that early modern man interbred with the other species of humanity or certain lineages simply died off.

I am sure the Neanderthals' interbreeding with the Cro-Magnons was out of pure survival. When living in such environments, early humans did not have time to learn about interpersonal intelligence or social intelligence. Today, humans have gone past the basics. We have created a new form of sociability through online means and services. Many educational documents and videos can be presented for all to learn from. School textbooks can be written and published once online. This saves many trees from being cut down for paper. Most importantly, it is much quicker to add revisions as the subject evolves.

Learning a language is another form of intelligence called linguistic-verbal intelligence. How well one expresses themselves is a means of this form of intelligence. Being linguistic is more than learning new languages, it is how you understand the culture of the people who speak it. Reading and writing are a part of this form of intellect. Being attached to a hive mind does not make one all-knowing. Learning is a process. I am sure the early man, as they came together, had to understand one another. It was not instant understanding. Today, human education is far more complex than it was for them.

This project will cover five major aspects covering the history of humanity regarding collective consciousness: 1. Archaeology. 2. Philosophy. 3. Anthropology. 4. Social Intelligent. 5. Sociology. Right now, scientists are starting to develop the ability to have a hive mind — the next evolution of humanity. The human mind can do far more than most may realize. Humanity has done so much since the Internet became public. The final frontier is not space. It lies within each one of us.

What is holding us back in life? It is what Sophia said, "Fear." When we fear new things, it hinders us from achieving on every level of our lives. Why do we fear in the first place? If no one or thing is directly attacking us what is there to fear? Our brain is designed to protect us. As I said, the early human species lived under pure survival. They had no luxuries at all. It would not surprise me if they wore any clothing at all. Think of how many animals they had to kill to skin them. It was hard enough to kill them for food.

When humanity became civilized or evolved into modern Homo sapiens, we started to advance rapidly. We first lived in small groups — close families. Later we learned the importance of creating tribes. Small cities evolved into larger ones. Today, we have many States in a given nation with a population of nearly 8 billion people living on one planet. We have connected around the world in real-time as if we all were in a large room. What do you think is the next evolution of humanity?

Despite the wars over thousands of years, the population still grows at alarming rates. Humanity had bad leaders and outright horrible ones, but the drive to collect ourselves has not been destroyed. Even pandemic after pandemic crossing through time and space all over the world had not put a dent in our drive to evolve our minds, bodies, and spirits.

How many people know how to think outside their brains? You read right. There is more to being a human being than thinking within our brains. Ever hear the saying, "Listen to your heart, your brain is stupid?" It is talking about that very thing. Like there are several bits of intelligence and Emotional Quotient or Intrapersonal Intelligence is one of them. A person with this ability can strongly focus on the mental and emotional state of themselves and others. Yes, it takes all of us to achieve things in life. Why do you think we have nearly 8 billion people on one planet?

We were meant to work together. Is the human race miserable or happy during and after a war? Everyone knows war is the failure of the human race not getting along with each other. That means any war can be prevented. Look at the social media platforms. Why are so many attacking it with false information, telling the masses it is useless and dangerous, and speaking against anything new and exciting? If more took up the responsibilities of pushing forward, then the corrupt would nearly not exist because they can't if we succeed.

Humanity has the right to feel. If we humans can understand the difference between our thinking brains and our feelings vs weak emotions, then we cannot truly be humans. How many can recall what it was like being a student in public schools? We were trained to believe if we only sat still and paid attention. No one learns that way. Employers want their employees to take the initiative. We cannot do that if we are trained to be puppets in a public schoolhouse. The only way to fully learn to be anything in life as human beings is to get messy while making mistakes and learn as each day progresses under the experts of educators — in public classrooms, in everyday life, and yes, even in homes.

8

CHAPTER 7

The next day, Sophia was with Zak and his family including his sister, Kyla.

Kyla asked, "You must have some strong ability to get my brother to..."

Sophia looked at him and said, "It was not me at all."

Kiara said, "Nonsense! Yes, my son chose to be a part of the hive mind even temporarily, but it was you who guided him. Never cut yourself short."

Zak said, "I am grateful too, Sophia. Kyla is starting to get interested."

His sister smiled, "Yes, I am."

Sophia nearly forgot why she came over. "I am here to help you practice. It is nothing more than what we have done already, and having us having our one-on-one connection helped you deal with what you will be doing now."

Zak smiled, "I thought as much. It was why I decided to connect in class earlier. It was what you did for us that helped me with this decision. I wonder if I would at all if we did not have our private connection."

Kiara said, "Zak's father and I have helped him a little, but you should help him with the rest. It was you that did this for him. Only you can train him to use it fully."

"I felt he understood I would do that for him. It was the sole reason why I cried for joy after he said he was ready." She looked at Kyla, "I believe you should be with us. If you are interested in being part of the hive mind, you will learn what it is about on this level."

Zak asked, "What do we need to do?"

"Being part of this hive-mind network is more than mere communicating or connecting to billions of minds. There is no real difference in how humanity has been a part of the collective consciousness. The only real advancements are from how we have used this advanced technology that has allowed us to share, communicate, and yes, learn who we are as individuals."

"You said before, it took you time to learn how others thought and feel before you could accept it all. What did you mean by that?"

"All experiences if not all life are based on how our brains metabolize it all. How I understand it, and before we were born, science had realized that reality is not real." Seeing Zak was getting a bit confused, "it is how our minds turn it all into what we all call, reality. It is no different in how we share ourselves through the hive."

Kyla asked, "Are you saying we have manipulated ourselves more than the religious fanatics?"

"Yes and no. They confused us surely enough, but the blind followers chose to continually be fooled which led them to believe in anything told." She paused, "that is why no one has been turned into a puppet or some other mindless being because there is a failsafe system to prevent it."

She asked, "How?"

"Because everyone else is connected simultaneously. It is not a perfect system, but if anyone gets confused or distorted, others will know about it. That is how that Indian Hindu monk could be there for me the other day. He knew how I felt and was the perfect person to guide me."

"So you get the right helper each time?"

Kiara said, "Yes and no. Since Sophia was that upset, through the hive network, he was able to know how easy it was for him to give her the right information in the right way."

Kyla looked confused, "The right way? Mom, what are you talking about?"

"Know this if anything I can teach you as your mother. A wrong thing done in a wrong way is wrong. A right thing done in a wrong way is wrong. A wrong thing done in the right way is wrong. Only through both premises being right can one have the right results."

Still confused, "Will this hive network allow me or anyone to know what is the right thing or whatever?"

Patrick answered, "That my daughter is a very good question. Connected to anything in life no matter how many have done before you do not make any of us perfect. Any one of us can make mistakes, make the wrong choices, etc." He paused for a brief moment, "think of being connected to the hive network as learning anything in life. We are not one huge mind. That would be impossible."

She asked her father, "How are you all connected? How can any mind be shared throughout the world as if we are standing in this room?"

Sophia answered, "That is why we are doing this project. Most don't know. On a basic level, it is far more than being connected to the Internet that we still use today. What I have learned is similar to what has been coined as the Wood Wide Web."

"OH MY! You mean the trees, plants, and all-natural life are connected too?"

Kiara answered, "Very much so, but to this day, we have not fully understood how. What we have going for us humans is barely a slither to what they have been doing for millions of years."

Before allowing that to consume her, Kyla said, "What does the past have anything to do with us today? Connected to the hive network or not?"

Her mother answered, "Everything. Children whether connected to the hive or not, go to school. Learning takes time. It is not a given. This technology that allows us to share our minds does not teach us anything. Like Zak, he has to be trained to use it to get the full benefit of being connected. No one loses or gains anything." She nearly saw the question in her daughter's expression, "that is right Kyla, our brains stay the same."

"There is a difference?"

Zak said, "I hope so. How I see it, the brain is physical where our mind is not."

With a confused look, "Say what?!"

Patrick said, "I do admit, it is a debatable thing. There is one thing scientists and philosophers agree on, they are different. It is how to this day no one can agree."

Sophia said, "What Bampás has told me regarding the philosophy part, think of it as a soul." It is the scientist that can't prove we have one."

Kyla grumbled, "That is stupid. Of course, we have one. How can we be self-aware?"

Her father threw it back at her, "But can you prove that? It is more than recognizing yourself in the mirror or a photo."

She grumbled again, "Why does everything in the blasted universe have to be proven?"

He smiled, "Exactly, my daughter. Exactly."

"I see why everyone is connected. How could the human mind and brain evolve? We argue over everything too much."

Her mother giggled, "How true, but we are learning even though true education must be done the old fashion way."

"I wonder if everyone did not argue over every little thing, maybe just maybe this hive mind network can educate in a whole new way. If the human mind is going to evolve from the craziness of the early 2020s, then maybe they are teaching in schools wrong."

Sophia liked that line of questioning. "That may be a good element to add to this project. Trust me, Kyla, you are ready to connect to the hive more than you realize."

At that moment she got a sharp eagerness to do that. She just stood there silently with no emotions. What seemed like several moments, was only a few seconds. Yes, the measurement of time has its reality — and it is not always linear. Finally, she said, "if you are going to train us both, I might as well."

Sophia smiled, "You are like your brother more than you realize."

Kyla smiled back, "I always knew being male or female does not make a person." She paused, "I know we were similar a great deal. It was I that helped him deal with his ordeal being connected with you."

She abruptly turned to look at him. She said, "Really!?"

Zak smiled warmly, "Sorry I did not mention that to you. We usually don't share intimate things with others. She got me to realize what you did for me was not the reason I got upset. It was how I thought before joining you in that intimate way."

Sophia asked, "How do you feel now?"

"A lot better, thanks to you. That is why telling you I was ready was the right thing to do — now rather than later."

"I know, my love. I felt that from you. It was why I cried in front of everyone." She turned to look back at Kyla, "you have a strong empathic ability. That is how I knew you two were so strongly bonded and nearly identical — mentally anyhow."

Kyla asked, "How will being connected change that status?"

"Good question. Asking such questions means you have a better understanding of collective consciousness." She paused, "are you ready."

She smiled, "Yes, I am."

As before, Sophia put out her left palm facing up. Suddenly a small cylinder appeared. After it did, "I can set it to the same length as your brother. It is up to you."

"I know what Zak told me, but I never knew one could be connected to the hive network temporarily."

"It is totally up to you, Kyla. If you want to wait longer to decide, no one will judge you for it."

With a positive expression, she said, "I want to do this. How excited Zak got..."

"That may be true, and I share your excitement for him. Everyone has a choice. It is a big decision. A lot has been said and shared with you, but what do you want to do?"

"Without blinking, I want you to connect me to this hive network... permanently."

Sophia asked Kiara and Patrick, "Any objections from you two? I know at her age, you have the final say."

Patrick said, "Yes, we do, but as you said, this is for Kyla to decide, and when she is sure of herself, as she is now, it is sealed and delivered."

She looked at Zak, "What about you, my love?"

"Believe it or not, I am linked permanently too."

"I thought I set it for five years for you? How?"

He smiled, "After class, Yeva and I had a good talk. That monk of yours joined us. After a good conversation, it was Yeva that set me on — permanently."

Kyla teased, "Well, are you going to connect me before you two kiss and caress each other passionately?"

Sophia turned around and said, "Please tilt your head, so I can put the Nanobots under your right ear."

Moments later, Kyla said, "I don't feel anything."

Patrick said, "Exactly! That is why we have been telling you, that nothing will change about who you were before the blending. It is why we have allowed Sophia to do this for you. She will be the one to train you how to flex your mind in this new environment."

Sophia said, "No one can use telekinesis or the other stuff from those old Hollywood movies and television shows. I am happy with all that went before I was born."

"What I learned in a media class in elementary school, those horror movies were C-O-R-N-Y!"

Her father replied, "If that can describe them."

Sophia said, "I'd rather read anyhow than watch a production of the same story."

Kyla asked, "What now. What do we need to learn to be truly a part of the hive mind?"

She smiled, "That is easy and hard. Let me put it this way." She paused to dramatize the moment. "unity over self."

Kiara asked, "Do you two understand that simple phrase?" Not giving them the chance to answer, "it is far more than the words themselves. It is what, why, and how we are all connected all around the world to this very day. It is also why everyone, including Sophia, is given the freedom to choose. Do you understand why that is so?" Seeing they did not fully understand, "that is why it is harder than easy."

Sophia said, "That is what I will be training you to understand. Don't worry, I, too, had a difficult time with it. That was why so many in the early 21st century had so much chaos. They did things 180 degrees the opposite by putting themselves, as individuals, over the whole."

****

Today, we don't need all the drama to fix our problems with the war in Ukraine, our multitude of issues facing our Constitutional Federal Republic in the United States of America, or anything in our personal lives. All we need is the right mindset. As Sophia said, UNITY OVER SELF! It is harder than you think, but at the same time, it should not be.

For the billions connected to their hive-mind network, the more that understood this simple statement, the better it is for everyone. Makes you wonder if ancient civilizations understood this, fewer wars would have been fought. Humanity could have had many advancements thousands of years earlier. Humanity may need to be connected like this today to fully understand this or at least learn what true collective consciousness means.

9

CHAPTER 8

U nity over self. What a basic concept, but one of the hardest things for humanity of any era to achieve. Do you think we would have learned something over the 77-Year War? Have you ever heard of it? What do they teach in schools these days? I bet you have heard of World War I, World War II, and the Cold War. What most may not realize — the end of WWI, started WWII. What ended that war started something that was not cold at all — the Cold War. From 1914 to 1991, these continual wars (with different names) lasted 77 years. Of course, how one ended the other did not just spark up all of a sudden. I will allow you to learn all about that in more detail on your own. War is not a part of this story.

What Sophia was concerned about with Scarlet Knox, at first, when people usually gather against something, they are a destroyer of unity. Sophia was happy to learn she was not like that at all. Recall what I just said about those wars. The Treaty of Versailles sealed the end of WWI, but how tight the restraints were on Germany years after, caused Adolf Hitler to take power and became ruler over Germany. He is the sole individual to start WWII. Even years after the world became a hive mind through advanced technologies, someone just as radical could start a war. The ones of hate over the ones connected would think they were pure humans and the disgusting enemy should be disconnected or die.

Ever heard of the Dark Ages/Middle Ages? The radical Christians thought they were superior to everyone. If you were not like them or a part of their clan, you were treated worse than a criminal — without any rule of law to protect anyone. Christian or any other religious tyranny is the worst kind of government. The Roman Catholic Church murdered thousands, and there was no one to stop them. How that was reversed — the Will of God had to turn things because this type of behavior is never taught in any religious text — even to this day.

Happily, Sophia will not have to train the minds of Zak and Kyla, but they appear not to know much about UNITY OVER SELF. S ometimes... no... a lot of times generations after generations, the young minds go soft. The eye of the tiger of learning diminishes. All the good qualities that earlier generations learned, drop, but not necessarily at the fault of the younger generation. These important aspects of life must be taught — no... trained in the minds of the new generation.

It is easy for many to say, HELP THE PEOPLE OF UKRAINE in the war with Putin, but because of the lack of understanding of The Treaty of Versailles, they will have no clue of the dangers of con-straining another nation too powerfully. It is why the United States of America is still the strongest Constitutional Federal Republic in the world. Under a true Democracy (a mob rule of 51 to 49), the USA would have been history a long time ago. I hope our lawmakers make these important and difficult decisions.

****

With Scarlet Knox sharing the wonders of what the hive mind is about and what Sophia Vitaloti's class project will bring, it was all over the news channels, weekly nighttime shows, and online social media platforms.

With her parents, Sophia said, "GOOD GRIEF. Why did Scarlet have to do that?"

Her father said with a smile, "If you do that good in life, what did you expect?"

She gave a huge sigh, "I know, Bampás." She paused and continued, "I don't want to be this popular." She paused again, "αυτό πάει πολύ γρήγορα. Γιατί είμαι σε βάθρο; Το μόνο που έκανα ήταν να σου κάνω αυτή την ερώτηση και την επόμενη στιγμή, ηγούμαι ενός τεράστιου έργου που μεγαλώνει κάθε στιγμή. Τι με κάνει κάτι που δεν είμαι — δημοφιλές; (aftó páei polý grígora. Giatí eímai se váthro? To móno pou ékana ítan na sou káno aftí tin erótisi kai tin epómeni stigmí, igoúmai enós terástiou érgou pou megalónei káthe stigmí. Ti me kánei káti pou den eímai — dimofilés?) / this is going too fast. Why am I on a pedestal? The only thing I did was ask you that question and the next moment, I am leading a huge project that is growing by the moment. What makes me something I am not — popular?"

He smiled, "Είσαι έτοιμη, κόρη μου. Έχετε μιλήσει στο πλήθος στο παρελθόν. Έχετε κάνει μεγάλα έργα όπως αυτό αν όχι μεγαλύτερα. Μέχρι να ανακαλύψετε τον πυρήνα αυτού που αντιμετωπίζετε, θα σας κερδίσει. (Eísai étoimi, kóri mou. Échete milísei sto plíthos sto parelthón. Échete kánei megála érga ópos aftó an óchi megalýtera. Méchri na anakalýpsete ton pyrína aftoú pou antimetopízete, tha sas kerdísei.) You are ready, my daughter. You have spoken to crowds before. You have done big projects like this if not bigger. Until you discover the core of what you are facing, it will win over you."

[They continued to speak in Greek]

"How do I do that?" She thought about it for a moment, "are you saying it is why I asked the question to begin with?"

"Believe it or not, my daughter, only you can ask and answer the questions of your life. Why did you ask me that? Was it something you read or heard about?" He waited for her to answer him. Since she didn't, he continued, "that my dear is why you are the head of the project. Ms. Noda Miyu knows what you are capable of. This Monk appears to understand you too. Why don't you understand yourself as they have?"

Suddenly she felt something deep in her. She realized it was not from the hive mind system because only she can fully understand herself. Finally, she blurted out in American English, "I wanted to know myself more from within than from the hive mind matrix through the experiences that only the ones that are not connected could answer."

"EXACTLY!"

As expected as Sophia walked out of the front door, there was a slew of news reporters who were ready to ask her questions. It was not until she saw her dear friends waiting for her to come to the podium. Zak said to her in her mind, "I have complete confidence in you, my love. Just be yourself, and let that guide you."

She smiled and walked up to the podium.

One news reporter asked, "How is the class project we all have been hearing about going?"

Sophia answered, "We all have just started it, so it will be a while before any strong results are shared."

"What is the main theme of this report?"

She looked quietly at Zak and Kyla Harris and back at the reporter, "As I have told these two yesterday, the main training to be a part of this hive-mind network of ours is unity over self. As we all know, we are individuals, but we must put the whole over ourselves or no good will come out of the bonding. It is different for everyone. It is as it should be. For the first time in human history, we have not had any wars or similar hatred over others. If anything I want to come out of this class project — for all to understand, that we can get along with each other if we are connected to this wonderful network of ours or not. Any walls between the haves and have-nots can join hands."

Another reporter asked, "So you are after world peace or something like that?"

"I first wanted to know why people have not connected. As I learned more about collective consciousness that had started nearly from the beginning of humanity, I started to understand what it was like to not be connected." She paused and continued, "I can't experience everyone's point of view — in which each one of our personal lives is governed. I believe I have experienced it enough to get a better reality of why a good many don't want to ever connect. Let me state that this project will never influence others to do what they don't want to do. Once it is completed, I hope we all can understand each other more."

The reporter smiled, "Sounds like world peace to me."

Sophia smiled back, "It could be, but that is up to who wants to make it that way. To the ones here that are not connected, we are not of one mind. We are complete individuals as we were before each one of us completely and freely chose to join this wonderful bond. I am talking to all of you today through the person you see. No one is not feeding me the words coming out of my mouth." She paused to look at Zak for a brief second, "my boyfriend, his sister, and other dear friends are here to support me. That is all."

A third reporter said, "What is your belief... if that is the right word... on being connected? You appear to be neutral with who chooses to be a part of our union."

"First, I want to state, me asking my Bampás... I mean daddy... long story why I chose that Greek word. Anyhow, I was not biased or thought the ones not connected were lower-class people. I never believed in the Caste System and never will." She paused, "that said, I never wanted to be disconnected because to this day, my life is much better." She looked at the crowd for a brief moment, "it does not mean your lives would be better or worse. My choices and yours are for each one of us to be responsible."

"But what is your opinion about being connected?"

She smiled respectfully, "I will not answer that directly because I don't want others to think they have to believe as I do. What inspiration I may give is for them to do as they wish. Believe it or not, I don't directly give any inspiration."

"Believe it or not, Sophia Vitaloti, you have done just that. We all would not be here if it was not for you."

"OH, MY GOD! He is right." She remembered what the monk said, 'Service is proof of real love. Service means the sacrifice of work and sacrifice of the fruit of work. The mother serves her child by the sacrifice of work like giving a bath, dressing etc., for years together continuously. The father serves the child by the sacrifice of the fruit of his entire hard work. It is a clear practical point that the proof of real love is the only service. If you serve your family, you love your family. If you serve the entire world, you love the creation, If you serve God, you love God and this is only devotion.' "Yes, you are right, this is my duty."

"It is because of your duty, we are here. You are young biologically, but believe me, you are more mature than everyone here."

Everyone cheered.

She just modestly stood there. She was not expecting this. All she did was ask a simple question.

Ms. Miyu's voice came to her head, "This is why I changed my class program. You are thinking why? You know sometimes the best questions get a huge answer. The spark came from you. If you were biased in any way, these reporters would not be with you. They are here because all over the media the world is witnessing what you are doing."

"OH, MY GOODNESS! Everyone knows?"

"They are watching you at this very moment. They are learning everything from you, Sophia."

"By me asking a simple question?"

"It takes nothing less. Put it this way. It's why you asked that made all the difference. You wanted to help others by guiding them to this very moment. The spark is from you. Find the light from within yourself and allow it to flow through you."

The same reporter asked, "But what is your opinion about being connected?"

"I have been connected since age nine. Before I did so, I learned all I can around age five. Since then, I have experienced no ill from all those that have been connected before me. As with everyone else, I guess, I did not feel anything different. It took time to learn how to understand the minds of billions around the world. When I learned about others, I learned more about myself than at any time in my life. All those years since I can't see how I could live without having my mind not be a part of everyone else. What I recently learned, all that I have done came from me. I partially understood this, but the more I learn about collective consciousness that has been going on since as far back as the Neanderthals, this is for everyone — in their way."

The reporter asked another question, "Through this class project that Ms. Noda Miyu, your instructor, said had everything to do with you, what are you saying to the world?"

Suddenly she realized the magnitude — it was her that started this all. She did not ask her father that question to be prejudiced. She saw it as if she was the one that was not connected and wanted to enlighten or allow understanding of what she had experienced since day one. She felt from within herself that light, and she wanted to give everyone the opportunity she had in her — this moment... this day. She answered, "I want the world, especially the ones that have not crossed into our world, the massive wonders and responsibilities of being connected to the hive mind." She looked more directly at the cameras, "you will never lose the person you are right now, but you will learn more of who you are in years to come."

Seeing everyone was quiet, she realized they wanted more from her.

"This project will talk a great deal about collective consciousness that has been going on since far before civilized mankind. We, humans, have gathered as a small unit. I would have to believe mostly family and close friends. As the populace grew, we learned to gather into tribes. Many, many years later towns, cities, states, and nations all over the world have. This project will gather information on why we have evolved into what we are today — one mind while being billions of individuals."

I believe the more we learn, the more we can grow as individuals, as a society, as a nation, and as one human race. I have learned more about different cultures and ways of life that I could never experience alone. I mean if I was never connected. That is why I asked Bampás." She gave a warm smile, "I mean my father. I have been calling him since not long after I have been connected. The word means father in Greek. I love languages and can speak several, fluently."

I want everyone that has not been connected, the chance to experience all that I have over my years. Can we learn outside the hive mind? Of course, we can. As I have said, I learned a great deal about it before I freely choose to do so. Since then, I have learned megatons more than my imagination could not understand. We are never meant to live alone. One is a lonely number. Humanity all around the globe has evolved for the better I dearly believe. Are we perfect? No! I wonder if we ever could find perfection, the end of our individuality if not the human race would end. Right now, a great deal of unity and understanding vs the wars we had for many, many centuries are at an end."

Through our one-hive mind unity, we are much better. I know I am a much better person than I would otherwise. I know one thing for certain, I could not expanded who I am today if I was not connected. I am gracefully humbled and grateful to be a part of this system. What started to be a simple question, turned into something I was not expecting. As I have said to my beloved boyfriend and his sister — Zak and Kyla Harris, Unity over self."

Since I said that, my resolve to complete my duty has strengthened. No matter the outcome, when this class project is completed, I know I have fulfilled this duty."

Another reporter asked, "Ms. Vitaloti, what is your duty?"

"Before we can help another, we must first learn to be the best we can. I am doing so right now. I hope it will be enough to complete this project. With the whole body of students, I know we all will." She paused, "my duty — answer my question I gave Bampás last week. The more I will learn, the more this class project will share that."

A reporter asked, "Are you worried if some don't connect, they will be like radicals of... say... January 6, 2021?"

"A very good question. Anyone can be stupid. None of us are perfect or close to it but have been connected for a good many years. Since no one is forced to join our hive mind — I wasn't. I could have joined a few years earlier. I first wanted to learn all I could. I hope that everyone will learn more once this project is completed than I did."

The questions went on for around twenty minutes longer. They are more or less general questions about who she was and believed. Everyone wanted to know her because she will lead a great many human minds — connected to the hive system or not. The final frontier is not space and the universe. It is what the human minds will share once they populate the stars in many generations.

What message will the future of humanity give if there are other lifeforms to share with? We may be the future generations to populate every planet that supports life as we know it on Earth. First, we must have the right mindset to achieve what is out there. We the people of Earth must be the blue beacon before we can learn how to travel and live safely throughout the stars.

10

— • —

Chapter 9

By now, if not before you started reading this story, you may be wondering how can all these minds be connected without losing one's individuality. Do you live in a town or city which is in a State? What about the nation you live in? Each of these and other groups we all congregate in have principles, and rules, if not laws to govern a society. Do you follow the majority if you believe it or not just to fit in? These questions define a collective. We do more in functioning as a group than as individuals — while holding our individuality. Confused? There is no reason to be.

Humanity has been living on what is termed, a collective consciousness for as long as humans (early man or modern) have been on this Earth. As this story has stated before, we have one to six percent Neanderthal genes in our bodies. What is so amazing, can early primitive mankind associate with one another? For them and us today, it is survival. Humans today have evolved with the many cultures and ways of life throughout time and space on one planet. From the trees, caves, towns/cities, States, and nations over thousands of years, we have nearly eight billion people alive today.

Duality is the concept of mind and body. The early man realized if they were to survive, they had to work with the Cro-Magnon.

With other early mankind living on Earth thousands of years ago, it is amazing we have any genome of Neanderthal in our bodies. Scientists and philosophers believe that both the mind and body are separate. The rest is debatable which I can't discuss with you now. I do not think anyone can do that. The point of this story is how it relates to a technical marvel of connecting the human brain to this hive network while keeping us as individuals as we were born to be. If you have not gotten the hint, the individual human mind is just as free. The human brain and mind are two different things. The biological life is just a taxi cab to carry the mind/soul of the individual.

For now, think of having billions of minds inner-connected with each other as having the brain, a new computer, connected to the Internet. Since the human brain can store around 2.5 petabytes, each brain can easily be a wetware of this new Internet — sharing information at will. That is one large storage of 20 billion petabytes. From ⅄ "In 2020, the amount of data on the Internet hit 40 zettabytes. A zettabyte is about a trillion gigabytes." Those huge numbers can blow my (not so big) pea-brain on the magnitude of how big the storage space if every human being were connected as such. The technology of connecting the human mind as a hive network is becoming a more scientific fact. As with anything, it is the application of achieving such a feat. To orchestrate the structure of that much data from every human mind, yes, calling it a feat is a petabyte understatement.

I believe it is not as hard as it may first appear. We learn things over the years of our lives. Our brain grows as well as our bodies. How we commit ourselves to a given society and different ones as we move physically from one place to another. We have been evolving under this type of living since day one on endless dimensions of our lives throughout time, space, and everything that has made us human beings that we have evolved into this very day.

If you only refer to human evolution from the moment we became civilized, then that would wow you across the planet; nevertheless, early man had created tools that are found all over the United States of America and elsewhere. Archaeologists have found many things to show the lifestyle of different eras. These were called lost civilizations. To this very day, medical science can't fully replicate how the ancient Egyptians mummified their dead. If humanity was connected to a hive mind then, maybe we could do all they have done if not more. If humanity was connected today, what can we pass down to generations after us in a few thousand years? The mind is a terrible thing to waste.

****

Another weekend approached and Sophia was sleeping in her bed. She had a dream of sorts, but it was not an ordinary one. This was real but much different than what the real world would understand as substantial.

A voice came to her head. Sophia thought the child's voice was real enough, but she never had spoken to this person before. She said, "Hello, it is great to talk with you. Believe it or not, I am dead and gone, but we have met many times before. Like all dreams, we usually forget those moments after we wake up. Go deep within your mind. We have talked before Ms. Vitaloti."

"Autumn... Autumn Heath? How?"

"That is a long story, but because I was the first mind to be connected to a hive system, I somehow survived Rett syndrome. From there, I lived onward... to this very day."

"WHAT? You never told me that."

"I know I have not. It is why I am talking directly to you. I had to help you along the way to be able to talk with you as I am now — while you are sleeping. No, you are not dreaming this, my dear Sophia."

"How? I did not think the dead could live this long?"

"I am dead as far as I once was in life as you know. I believe my mind was kept alive to wander through the complexity of what you call a hive mind. Trust me, no hard drive or device is allowing you all to achieve what you have been doing. Each one of you is that hard drive... maybe it should be called a live-ware drive. It took many years to find you, but I stayed in your mind when I did."

"I know I sound like a broken record, but how? How can you enter my brain?"

"No one can enter your brain, sweet Sophia, especially yours. Believe it or not, no human brain is connected. The mind is not a physical thing. It is why people before could connect through love, commitments, and other means if they realized it or not."

"If that is the case, how did you survive Rett syndrome?"

"That is complex, and if it were not for a slow deterioration of my condition, I would not have lived past four years old. I was lucky that medical science created a set of integrated circuits that were placed in my head, I would not be talking to you. This technology communicated with a very sophisticated artificial intelligence. Before I was almost 12, that was not enough. My mental growth was not getting worse, but neither was it improving." She paused to allow Sophia to absorb all she told her before continuing, "daddy was a highly skilled neurosurgeon, and he and his team developed a means for human minds to connect — a basic technology to what you all have today. Anyhow, he thought to have other minds communicate with my mind to help me strengthen my condition. It did."

She interrupted, "If you don't mind answering, how many human minds did it take?"

"That is why I am talking to you about this, sweetie. I am ready to tell you everything. At first, it was the immediate family. Later, it was the neighbors that had a great love for both my parents. As I got older, more joined this crude mental connection."

"So that is why we have our hive mind network all around the world."

"Yes and no. As the technology became more successful the smaller technology became. It became cheaper and more connected to help cure other neurological disorders in the United States. Curing those types of diseases did not stop with this new unparalleled evolution of humanity. It took time, but after a few decades, nearly the world population was connected. As the technology continued to advance, they started to use Nanobots technology."

"WOW! Who would have guessed." Sophia paused, "why me? You said once you found my pea-brain... I mean mind, you settled. What makes me so special?"

"Foremost, you are not a pea-brain, but if you did not start to think outside your brain, you would not be the person you are today, and it had nothing to do with you connecting to the hive. You have been destined to be the leader of your generation to teach them about the beginning, and it is so much more than what I have just told you. Yes, it started with me, but afterward, it skyrocketed beyond science fiction."

Immediately, Sophia woke up. She felt something enter her heart that told her something unique in her entire life. She blurted out,

"This is my duty." She got out of bed and got dressed. She knew she could not go back to sleep with this running in her. After walking out of her room, she quietly exited onto the front yard to rock in the porch swing. She did so until she felt her love, wake up that morning. She had to tell him everything.

When she felt he was up through monitoring him, she waited before he was more awake. She waited until he showered and got dressed.

He said, "I hope you liked seeing me naked and taking a shower?"

She giggled, "I like looking at you... no matter what you have on or don't." She paused, "there is no hurry, but we need to talk. I had an interesting conversation with someone when I was sleeping."

After telling him every detail, he said, "HOLY COW! I suggest you talk to your mother about her. I am sure there are records or something. If anything it could be a journal or diary from her. Of course, she would not have known you then, but you may learn something. If this neurological disorder hit her..."

"Good point, love. Sorry, I do tend to interrupt a lot."

"No problem. Yeva told me all about that."

She got upset, "I will bust that Ukrainian ass of hers. She had no right..."

He giggled, "It is fine, love. It was more in jest than anything."

"She was afraid I would tear up her ass for her."

"She thought of that and told me it can't be straightened out."

She laughed in her mind, "See you soon."

"If we can't physically, anyhow, I will let you know."

"The question is why me?"

"If Ms. Miyu knew to make you the project leader, then the more you learn, the more you can answer that question." He paused, "you took charge of helping me before I finally connected. You helped Kyla. We both are doing great with what you taught us that day."

"I am only 17. Only adults in their 50s usually make such dynamic achievements."

"You have nevertheless. I think you may need to accept and believe what you have accomplished."

She felt her mother was looking for her. She said, "I better get in the house. There will be a great chance I will be in the library later on. See if you can meet me there."

Pippa said, "I talked to Zak's parents, I will pick you up in a bit."

Zak said, "I will be ready then."

"No hurry. I am the caretaker, so I make my hours. Of course, I am there a great deal, but please don't rush."

"Thanks, Ms. Vitaloti. See you both then."

Moments after entering the house, her mother asked, "What was that hype telling him you are not worthy of what you have accomplished? You know age has nothing to do with it. There have been in American History if not World History of people younger than you that have done great things."

"Until now, I did not know what all I had done. It has overwhelmed me that I have done all this."

Her father said, "Ακόμα σκέφτεσαι ότι δεν τα έχεις κάνει όλα, κόρη μου. (Akóma skéftesai óti den ta écheis kánei óla, kóri mou.) / You are still thinking you have not done them all, my daughter."

When he spoke in Greek with the best accent, she realized he was not upset with her as in scolding her, but what he said still had importance. She answered, "Ναι, Μπαμπάς. (Nai, Bampás.) / Yes, Bampás." She thought of the right words to say, "είναι απλώς συντριπτικό. (eínai aplós syntriptikó.) / it is just overwhelming."

Her mother smiled and spoke in Greek, "Πάντα φοβόσουν τα νέα πράγματα. Λέω τον φόβο μέσα σου όταν η κ. Miyu σου έδωσε αυτήν την ανάθεση ως επικεφαλής αυτής της τάξης. Συνειδητοποίησε, αυτό προοριζόταν να το κάνεις. (Pánta fovósoun ta néa prágmata. Léo ton fóvo mésa sou ótan i k. Miyu sou édose aftín tin anáthesi os epikefalís aftís tis táxis. Syneiditopoíise, aftó proorizótan na to káneis.) / You were always terrified of new things. I saw the fear in you when Ms. Miyu gave you this assignment as head of this class project. She realized this was meant for you to do." She paused and spoke the rest in English, "want to know something, I know you can handle it, and you will enlighten everyone that will read it when it is posted online."

After thanking them both, she told them both what Autumn Heath told her when she was sleeping.

Pippa said, "I know a great deal about her."

Sophia looked puzzled, "How come I don't?"

Nikolas said, "What does that have to do with it? You know one has to acquire knowledge on their own. As Autumn told you, we are connected to this hive because each one of us is a part of it. From what I understand, it was not like this. Think of it like the old sneakernet technology."

"You mean physically carrying a floppy disk or the like to the destination?"

"Exactly that, my daughter. It was no different when you and Zak had your private, one on one connection. You simply shared through your own autonomous or self-governing system."

"If that is the case, Bampás, how can we be connected all over the world with billions of minds?"

Her mother answered, "I will give you the resources you and Zak will digest. For a simple approach, think of it as how we can today use the Internet in this state, the nation, and the world. I will not say more than that. You will have to learn this for yourself."

11

— ◆ —

Chapter 10

By the International Rett Syndrome Foundation, Rett Syndrome is "a rare genetic neurological disorder that affects 1 in 10,000 females (and even more rarely in males) and begins to display itself in missed milestones or regression at 6-18 months. Rett syndrome leads to severe impairments, affecting nearly every aspect of life: the ability to speak, walk, eat, and breathe easily. The hallmark of Rett syndrome is near constant repetitive hand movements while awake." Right now, there is no cure for this neurological disorder.

Could human minds cure diseases by having blueprints of healthy individuals incurring any disease like this one through a hive mind network? Today, no, but who knows what tomorrow will bring? Until we fight for science and future advancements, the change is minimal. Instead of thinking of what may see what would have happened if science did not exist at the stages, it is now on every level of human advancements. On a more personal note, where would you be if it was not for the hard work that put you in the very existence of your life? If you have not worked hard, start now. There is no better time to begin.

A collective consciousness of people can't succeed without individuals. When one light goes out in a string of Christmas lights, the whole string can stop working. For 500 lights or whatever, that is a lot of bulbs someone has to go through to find the one that does not work. Those lights work like a hive mind. Yes, that dead bulb does not light the whole tree, but when all of them work in unison, it does make a memorable holiday. General Patton said, "Individuality is a bunch of horse crap." When we sit on our butts, nothing is done as family unity, society, or nation. If we work together for science, one day, we can cure all diseases on Earth, and maybe end the future of pandemics.

Could a hive mind system be the driving force to cure such diseases as Rett Syndrome? We are not going to know until we do a better job in our daily life. If we can have 1 to 6% genome of the Neanderthals in our bodies, create many societies, cultures, and all the rest with a population of nearly 8 billion, I believe we can do more than cure diseases if every human mind was connected. Imagine if humanity had a hive-mind system thousands of years ago. Think about what could be accomplished. In all the ages of humanity and their evolutions, we could do endless more if we could join our minds today. What could have been shared — including the possibility of reprogramming bad genetics through such mind technologies by good genomes from other people?

No progress has succeeded on the backs of individuals. It takes more than a simple team. It takes a collection of humans. As it had been done before to make reality happen. Even things created by accident — like penicillin. It took a team of people to achieve it. Why grades never excel students. Only failure does. When a team of scientists fails, they learn from their mistakes and move on. If a nation fails, the voters remove the lawmakers and replace them with ones that can do that job. It does not take one lawmaker but hundreds. Very few monarchs are recorded in history as great. Through an oligarchy, the people always suffer. Every free nation succeeds by the individuals that become one with their nation's government.

Under the United States of America, WE THE PEOPLE is a form of collective consciousness that forms a hive mind on what they want their nation to become. How they vote, act after election day, and live in their community defines how their future will shine. I can easily see that we have already created a hive mind. What is next in the evolution of humanity is to technically connect our minds to become greater than we are today — a more perfect humanity.

****

Being outside once more, Sophia thought over all the extensive research at the library, and she ached to write another message for the project. Since everyone around the world will be reading and examining their finished project, she thought about how to enlighten everyone. Yes, most are connected to their hive mind system, but it does not necessarily mean they are connected... "How can I say it? Should I say, 'connected as they should,' be a cliché or outright corny? I need a word... NO, AN IDEA, that means so much more."

After getting up from the porch swing, she walked into the house. When she entered her room, she sat at her desk. Once she loaded up the word processor, she started to write...

~~~~~

This huge class project started, if I realized it or not, with a question. Like any good idea, it always starts as a question. It concerned me... NO THAT WAS NOT the word... WORRIED. Yes, I was worried about the ones that were not connected to our hive system, but I
~~~~~

was more so for the billions that have already because... we are not whole as we may believe.

Everyone, throughout human history, has always been concerned about the majority having all the right answers. In reality, it is usually the minority we should be listening to. I can't say, they have all the right answers either, but if the majority listens to them more, everyone would understand more about life. The majority if not all of us need to listen more than beat our chest and give the answers we know that are wrong. That is right, I put myself up on the same stage. How quickly I want to speak and think I can share what is in my little brain. Later, deep down, I realized I knew nothing. As Socrates said, "The more we know, the more we realize we know nothing."

Back to this project — the Neanderthals don't exist anymore other than the possible 1 to 6 percent genome still in most humans today. I don't know much if any medical benefits are risks of having their genome in our bodies, but in those many thousands of years, it shows that we are all connected as one human race. I read from an article on January 24, 2021, from www.livescience.com "Most scientists recognized at least 21 different human species." Today, we only have one, but we are far more divided than this count of past humans.

I know, we are individuals, and we should stay that way. At the same time, we are destroying ourselves. It makes me wonder if more were connected to our hive mind network because we had too much hatred going on in the early 21st century. Reading other materials from mom's library, especially about that era, how are we still a nation today... while still calling ourselves the United States of America? They teach us in school, there are more good people than bad ones. After reading about that part of our history... I don't know.

Both Zak and I have read — the reasons generations before us, had uniquely different reasons to connect and stay connected to what we call the hive network. What makes our generation so different? Dammit to hell with who writes our history books. The outright horrible part of that history may be the most important thing we should apply to how we live today, so we can have a more perfect union of humanity if we are connected or not.

Do I want to be disconnected? If we don't learn what is required, all of us could do more damage if we were never connected at all. Where would I be right now, if I did not have that Indian monk talk to me alone and later on to the entire class after Zak was truly connected? Yes, I was the one to do that and not Yeva. She told both of us when she helped us with the research. I am going off-topic again. Let me finish this before I am late for school.

If all of us don't learn all that we have done in the library, Zak's connection could be cut off for good. There is more to being an individual and a team of humanity than what most know and realize about how we have billions of minds connected. In what we students have been working on so far, the main underlying theme must be to give that knowledge to everyone. I now understand why this one-class project will be given to the public after we complete it. Since this was given to me by a question I uttered, it will be my duty to make sure this gets done.

~~~~~

After proofreading what she wrote, she sent a copy to Ms. Miyu. Sophia picked up her book bag and left her room.
~~~~~

As she was in the passenger seat of her mother's car, Ms. Miyu said in her mind, "□□□□□□□□ (Ohayō, Sofia) / Good morning, Sophia."

"□□□□□□□□ (Ohayō, Noda Mi yu) / Good morning, Noda Miyu"

She continued in English, "That was a great article you sent. I will place it with the other paper you wrote."

"I am sure I wrote more than I should. As I wrote, I tend to babble a great deal."

Ms. Miyu said with certainty, "When I say it will be presented, I meant all of it. What you wrote wasn't an essay or other important document. Both times you wrote from your heart."

With worry in her mental voice, "You mean something bad could happen to Zak's connection?"

"Not at all. With your love for him and his love for you, nothing bad will happen." She paused, "there is a lot on your mind. I don't need our hive-mind technology to feel that in you. Trust me, this is your duty, Sophia. You have and will do great."

"That might be it. If this is my duty, I hope I can fulfill this project."

"There is no hope about it. Don't be so overwhelmed by what you are doing. Know that every student will do their part and then some."

It was not long before Sophia's mother pulled near the front door of the school. She said to her daughter, "Ms. Noda Miyu is right, you have done your best, and you will continue to do so, baby. I can't be prouder than I am of you."

She smiled, "Thanks, mom. I would like to know how you knew we were talking?"

"That is easy, my daughter, you have a great mind. Where else would a librarian be?"

They hugged dearly before Sophia exited the car to start the day.

****

It was not until the three were in the cafeteria that they had their first conversation since entering the school building that morning.

Somova always had that perfect Russian accent that Sophia loved, "How was your day?"

She got the message and realized they knew what she wrote and sent it to Ms. Miyu. Sophia answered, "Scared out of my mind." She told them about Autumn Heath.

Yeva replied, "I know about that, sweetie; we had a discussion about that in the library." She giggled, "I am happy our mental communication did not talk too loud as we were in that library."

Somova said, "Girlfriend, you are full of crap."

All three of them laughed.

Yeva said, "Guilty as charged."

Somova asked, "What scares you about Autumn, I would be tickled pink knowing I had someone in my head that came from a distant past."

Sophia sighed, "Why me? What makes me so special? She pulled a computer tablet out of her bag. After opening the file, she allowed them both to read what she sent Ms. Miyu this morning."

Both of them were amazed by what she wrote.

"You are kidding me! I have reread that several times, and I do not see how you are dumbfounded over it."

Yeva said, "I knew I should have busted your ass the other day — especially what you said in our Sociology Class on the first day."

"SHUT UP, YOU. You can't bust my ass even if I let you do it."

She acted like she was upset, "If you are thinking Autumn Heath was a figment of your imagination, you need your head examined." After a brief moment, she smiled, "then I will bust that ass of yours."

Sophia laughed, "Yeah, right."

Somova said, "You wrote this because you believe Autumn Heath talked to you. I don't know how she could have survived living in this mental matrix. She was something special, and so are you, my dear friend."

****

As the time came close, Sophia was becoming more nervous and excited to start the day in her Sociology Class. As usual, she was always early. Before walking in, she swallowed her emotions. She said, "□□□□□□□□□(Kon'nichiwa, Mi yu-san.) / Good afternoon, Ms. Miyu."

She smiled, "□□□□□□□□□□□□□□□□ (Kon'nichiwa, Sofia Bitaroti-san.) / Good afternoon, Ms. Sophia Vitaloti."

When she addressed her by her full name it was important. She stood at a semi-attention stance."

Seeing that, Ms. Noda Miyu grinned slightly, and said in English, "Please have a seat. As you have expected, today's class will be quite different." As she was walking to her desk, she continued, "because you reacted in the way you should, you know more than Japanese but our customs. You are very intellectual for your age. How you have been behaving, what you have written in your two letters for this project, and your actions now, you are proving to me, you are the best to lead this project, but you can't do it alone. Even the whole student body will need outside help."

Sophia in excitement said, "You knew about Autumn Heath?"

Ms. Miyu said, "Believe it or not, I did not know a single thing about her... until your mother shared all she had in the library she works at."

Just then two people walked into the classroom. One person was Principle Lydia Day; the other was someone Sophia never met in her life.

Ms. Day said, "Sophia, please let me introduce you to Alexandra Rosa. She is one of several ancestors of Autumn Heath."

The new arrival said, "Please call me Alexa or Alexandra."

Trying to get a grasp on what is going on, she asked, "Please excuse my asking. You and your family are responsible for keeping Autumn's mind alive? You being here, I take it, you know about her talking to me when I was sleeping?"

"Yes, I do. There is a great deal of why everyone is connected to what you call a 'hive mind.' In all due respects, it should be called a colloquial mind."

She looked puzzled, "A what?"

Ms. Miyu said, "A colloquium is a collection of deep thinkers collecting themselves by all means possible, like essays and other documents to discuss a specific topic." Our network is open to all and shares all, but as you recently wrote, not many realize this. You might say, we all have, in our way, fallen into our comfort zones even being connected. What I am saying... many have fallen in their individuality too deeply while forgetting they are connected."

Sophia said, "I was afraid of that."

Alexa said, "Trust me, Sophia, it is not as bad as it may appear, but you have stirred things in the right direction. This project you are in charge of..." Sophia looked at her instructor and back. Alexa smiled, "oh, she did not tell me or Ms. Day. I saw that in your eyes.

Your soul gave it away. You are a natural leader. That may be a bit scary, but you are one nevertheless."

An idea came to her head like an electric shock, "Are you saying, by me asking Bampás — I mean my daddy, that question, sparked me in being this leader?"

She looked deep into her eyes while at a distance from her, "It was your natural leadership that got you to ask your Bampás that question that sparked how things are evolving this very day." She studied what she was thinking and feeling. Before giving her the chance to speak, "that is why Autumn talked to you that morning."

Sophia asked, "Did she survive Rett Syndrome?"

Alexa smiled, "Yes, she did. I was not told how old she was when she died, but I understood, it was well in her adult years. As you may have expected, her mental and physical vigor was not fully developed, but yes, she survived it."

Running through her thoughts, "She wanted her mind to be in the hub of it all. She was the one to help expand what we have today?"

Alexa looked at Sophia's instructor, "I can see why you got her to be in charge of this project."

Noda Miyu gave a full smile to the point of laughing, "You have not experienced half of what she can achieve." She looked straight at her, "and it has nothing to do with being part of this colloquium mind system of ours."

Alexa said, "Know this if anything — being connected does not change or make you. Only through hard work can you achieve. Yes, you can learn from everyone, but what you have done and will do is completely in your hands. This colloquium does not turn people into zombies or drones. As you have expected, they are doing that to themselves... by themselves."

Sophia cursed out loud, "What can I do to help?"

Ms. Day said, "That is why I immediately accepted Ms. Noda Miyu's new class curriculum. Through your question you asked your Bampás, you ended up being the answer to your question."

12

CHAPTER 11

Y ou have been reading that Sophia has a duty if not a deeper purpose which has led to this class project. Generally, the word, duty means, a moral or legal obligation; a responsibility. With our protagonist, it is much more. As each one of us was meant to be alive — we have our part to play in the vastness of life. With Sophia, she will lead a whole planet of people to greatness, but she can't do it alone. If that is the case, why have billions of people alive at the same time?

Like a cog in an old fashion clock, we are to work as one in everyday life. Sophia's duty started with a simple question that has an impact that will light up everyone through the colloquium — Alexandra Rosa referred to as the hive mind network. If it helps, think of this hive-mind network as a college curriculum. In regards, it is an advanced system of learning and sharing of knowledge.

We may not know the full history of why or how every human being is now mentally connected to a colloquium of the vast undertaking of pansophy, but what this young female has in mind... could fulfill what Carl Sagan said about our planet and its inhabitants by having it expand throughout the universe, "Our planet is a lonely speck in the great enveloping cosmic dark. In our obscurity, in all this vastness, there is no hint that help will come from elsewhere to save us from ourselves."

As we have gun violence in America far beyond recorded history, hate, racism, and chaos in every direction, a 17-year-old female asked her father a question, which created a spark that is right now, traveling at light speed to the worlds that are out there to witness. There is a great deal for all to do on Earth before every living thing in the universe can bear witness to Earth's greatness, but it is on the right trajectory.

Sophia Vitaloti is not the appointed leader, like some queen bee over some hive, but she could be so much more. Not all leaders control like in a military unit. The best ones realize, to lead a mass of people like a nation or the world, everyone must do their part. General Patton told troops on June 5, 1944, "This individual heroic stuff is pure horse s---. The bilious bastards who write that kind of stuff for the Saturday Evening Post don't know any more about real fighting under fire than they know about f---ing!"

Sophia will in time wake up a lot of mindful lazy individuals that have once again, fallen into their deep comfort zones. Her authority is not like a General, but a great leader can allow an entire army to do things in war far better than they would otherwise. The energy of the mind is what moves mountains. Her skills will do just that for every human mind in this vast colloquium.

What is our purpose in life? Can that be defined? Spirituality like Hinduism is more of a walk of life than a religion. How is that different from religion? Let's define both of them. Religion means a group or organization that practices a set of standards. Sadly, throughout human history, this thing called religion has been cor-rupted by many over the years. Dictatorship always reigns supreme.

"Absolute power corrupts absolutely." On the other hand, Spirituality, or a walk of life, allows the individual to decide the standards of living after learning from the educators of any number of practices.

In Sophia's case, she has and will use her own experiences to achieve what was given to her. Who gave her this duty? The Indian monk? What about Noda Miyu, her sociology instructor? Was she born with this? It was her free will to ask her daddy/Bampás the question. Asking that question did not spark anything. Sophia could have scrapped the whole thing. Because she held her head high, everything built her obligation that will carry this class project to everyone around the world. Everyone will benefit from it beyond the imagination. After everyone reads the final project, they will finally realize why they all have been connected as one human race — not because billions of minds are interacting, but because they will learn how to do so in ways never fully understood.

Sophia's duty—reach out to every mind in this hive-mind network beyond its original design. For starters, they will interact as their brains do in their bodies. As they evolve, they will come to realize, they should have done this on day one being a part of the hive mind network but too afraid to flex their mental muscle.

****

Ms. Noda Miyu waited until every student entered the classroom before introducing their new guest.

Alexandra Rosa said, "I am sure by now, you all have heard about Autumn Heath. I am the CEO of the government agency that is organizing the very reason why you are connected to what you call a hive mind network. As I told Sophia, it's much more. We call it a colloquium. As you know, it means a place where experts of the highest caliber meet. Referring to billions connected to such a place

— for a better word, a seminar would not truly define it. I like to think of it as a global stoa — yes where the word stoic came from. This does not make us such philosophers; nevertheless, you share information of all kinds — directly or indirectly."

Sophia is the leader of this project — you are all undertaking be cause... believe it or not, she sparked it. Before she asked her father that question, she had in her heart the concerns of all involved — the ones that are not connected and the billions of humans who are."

Abigail Perry who is in charge of the philosophical part of the project raised her hand to speak. When Alexa gave the right signal, she said, "Are you referring to the relationship between the lawmakers and the citizens of such a government?"

"Yes and no. What I am referring to is what this project is about — not necessarily politics; though, believe it or not, it could have everything to do with it. If the people no matter what nation they live in and who governs them, this colloquium or stoa is about humanity as a whole. Like our nation is still governed by WE THE PEOPLE. One of many failures recently in the early 21st century was caused by the lack of responses from the whole of such people. As I said, this is not about anything political, but how humanity as a whole should come together."

Abigail looked hard at Sophia and said, "I see why you are in charge." She looked back at Alexa, "she is the type that would know how to help. She had done so with nearly all of us students on this campus in one way or the other."

Ms. Miyu said, "EXACTLY! That is why she is in charge."

At every student desk, there was sitting a small notebook-type computer but more advanced than anything known of the early 21st century. Ms. Miyu walked to her computer at her desk and sent the same document that Sophia recently wrote.

After Yeva reread it, she said, "I admit, I have read this a few times already, but each time, I felt my face drop in awe over what my dearest friend wrote."

Everyone said similar things.

Sophia said, "If we don't learn to be the people we should be — connected to our stoa or not, we could lose what and why humanity around the globe started this endeavor. In the grand scale of things, it is barely a drop in the bucket of how long we have been connected." She paused briefly, "think of the ones who have not — as the minorities. I am concerned these people will be treated horribly like racism or other bigotries. For the many who are connected, I feel they are too far in their comfort zone — like us Americans used to be in the low voting turnouts over the decades. They have allowed the corruption to build up without giving a damn about their inaction to stop it."

Cooper Marsh, the leader of the social intelligence group said, "I have to agree with you, Sophia. From what my team and I have gathered, we were terrified over how close we came to collapsing as a Constitutional Federal Republic. I take it you are concerned we could fall now?"

"Yes, I am. The political side of this project should be more on our government's history. Despite our Founding Fathers being racists, bigots, and yes, slave owners, they created our government as we have it today. Yes, we have made a lot of changes over the recent years, but the foundation of what they created in 1788 still holds. I believe we need to have something as strong all around the globe. How that can be easy and hard. Regarding this important stoa of ours, there are three philosophical principles: the responsibility of knowledge, the responsibility of how we conduct ourselves with our humility and integrity, and the responsibility of how we govern ourselves including our Republic. We must through this project reinforce the foundation of our understanding of why we have connected our minds. It is not a hive mind but a colloquium. Alexa's company is responsible for a computer gateway if I understand it right."

Alexa smiled at how brilliant this young woman has shown at this moment. She answered, "Yes, that is right. It is more to it for each human brain to store and share information, but all our brains can learn and store tons of information. Our gateway, as Sophia eloquently named it, is simply a means of allowing a better flow throughout the metropolitan area, the ability to share through other autonomous systems, and yes, the rest of the world. Think of it as a means to have brain waves travel all over the world."

Sophia asked, "I hope I am not being rude in asking this question, but why was Autumn attached to me? What I recall from her when I was a child, it was like dreams. All of a sudden she was communicating with me when I was sleeping."

"That I can't answer. She can communicate with anyone at any time. Know this about her if anything at all. Her mind was always intelligent and sharp. Even at a young age, she kept herself entertained. I was told, it was why she could adapt to being connected to the artificial intelligence that kept her going before other humans helped out by doing the same."

Zak said, "In all the time I have known you, Sophia, you are very intelligent and sharp-minded as well."

Ms. Miyu said, "□□□□□□□□□□ (i no naka no kawazu taikai wo shirazu) / A frog in a well knows nothing of the sea."

"□□□□□□□ □□□□□□□□□□□□□□□□□□□□□□□□□□□□ (Yareyare-da ze! Watashi ga kaerunara, watashi wa kyodaina ido ni iru ni chigai arimasen.) / Good grief! I must be in a huge well if I am the frog."

Principle Lydia Day replied, "It has nothing to do with the well or the sea, □□□□□□□□□□ (Sofia Vu~itari-san) / Ms. Sophia Vitaloti.

"Okay, what..."

Zak said, "This is a lot on you, and I assure you, every one of us here will help you. We know you can't carry this load all by yourself."

Yeva said, "That is correct, girlfriend." She paused, "since you have a lot to work on, let me help you with the Sociology part of this project. I and Somova Angela Victorovna will help you."

Ms. Miyu said, "Since this project will be online after it is completed, I will allow you to have outside help, but you all must do your part."

Jorgie Watts said, "It will take at least all of us to do this project. After my team has done a good deal of research, we want to go beyond what is required of us."

Everyone else declared the same thing.

Alexa said, "Since Principle Lydia Day told me about a questionnaire for people to fill out, I would like to be in charge of it. With my advanced understanding, I would be a qualified person."

Ms. Miyu smiled, "Yes, you would. I would like for the class body to read it before you distribute it if you don't mind."

"Not at all. I fully understand."

Sophia shared her anxieties with everyone.

Yeva asked, "Ти добре, подружка? (Ty dobre, podruzhka?) / Are you alright, girlfriend?"

"Я в порядку, я думаю. Це дуже багато, щоб прийняти. Я не знаю, чи зможу я це впоратися. (YA v poryadku, ya dumayu. Tse duzhe bahato, shchob pryynyaty. YA ne znayu, chy zmozhu ya tse vporatysya.) / I am fine, I think. This is a lot to accept. I don't know if I can handle it."

She smiled, "У вас це вийде, тому що ви не будете самотні. Ти мій найдорожчий друг, і я буду поруч з тобою. (U vas tse vyyde, tomu shcho vy ne budete samotni. Ty miy naydorozhchyy druh, i ya budu poruch z toboyu.) / You will make it because you will not be alone. You are my dearest friend, and I will be there for you."

"Спасибі. Ти мені потрібна більше, ніж ти знаєш. (Spasybi. Ty meni potribna bil'she, nizh ty znayesh.) / Thanks. I need you more than you know."

Yeva looked at the instructor, "She will be fine. She is stressed out a bit. A lot has been happening to her."

Ms. Miyu smiled at Sophia, "There is another proverb I would like to share with you if I may." After the nod, she said, "□□□□□□□□□□ (anzuru yori umu ga yasushi) / "It's easier to give birth than to think about it."

She knew the meaning very well. She said, "□□□□□□□□□□□□ □□□□□□□□□□□□□□□□□□□□□□□□□□□□□□□□ (Arigatō-gozaimashita. Shinpai shi sugite iru wakede wa arimasenga, takusan toriireru koto ga dekimasu.) / Thank you. It is not that I am over worrying, but a lot to take in."

Alexa asked Sophia, "How many languages can you speak?"

Yeva answered, "It is a lot more than speaking the several she knows, but she can understand the meaning behind the words, phrases, and proverbs." She paused, "I was told this had nothing to do with her being connected."

Alexa said, "Trust me. Anything we learn has nothing to do with the technologies we are connected to. We all can use the Internet as it was done in the early 21st century. You, I, or anyone else has to learn things like everyone else. I was just flabbergasted on how intelligent she is showing us right now." She looked dead-centered at Sophia, "if that does not answer your question about how Autumn Heath found you at a very early age of your life, nothing will."

13

— ◆ —

Chapter 12

What is a historical figure? Nine out of ten, they are a damn lie. Who writes the school's history books, documentaries, nonfiction books, etc.? They are usually people controlled by politicians, small groups, and others who do not care about truly presenting the facts. In a CNBC article Published Thu, September 20, 2018, 1:03 PM EDT, The Texas Board of Education voted to remove Hillary Clinton and Helen Keller from the school curriculum, shared, "held a preliminary vote to streamline social studies curriculum standards in all public schools. That included the removal of several historical figures, including Hillary Clinton and Helen Keller."

Public schools in America today barely teach anything because to control the young minds who could outright vote them out of office, they have to be completely ignorant of not only American History but key important aspects of human history throughout the world. After the 1960s rebellion, lawmakers made sure they could not achieve anything close to repeating what is required by the Declaration of Independence and the Preamble of the Constitution of the United States of America. Each one of us has the right to peacefully protest against corruption. Mass shootings by the White

Power Movements, and all the rest, are not any form of peaceful protest.

~ ~ ~ ~ ~

When in the Course of human events, it becomes necessary for one people to dissolve the political bands which have connected them with another, and to assume among the powers of the earth, the separate and equal station to which the Laws of Nature and of Nature's God entitle them, a decent respect to the opinions of mankind requires that they should declare the causes which impel them to the separation.

~ ~ ~ ~ ~

~ ~ ~ ~ ~

We the People of the United States, in Order to form a more perfect Union, establish Justice, insure domestic Tranquility, provide for the common defence, promote the general Welfare, and secure the Blessings of Liberty to ourselves and our Posterity, do ordain and establish this Constitution for the United States of America.

~ ~ ~ ~ ~

How many understand these two paragraphs, less alone the documents they came from? If most cannot answer either question or both, the corruption has already begun without realizing the damage. This type of corruption was done by people who want the government of the United States of America to be an oligarchy. Plato said, "Dictatorship naturally arises out of democracy, and the most aggravated form of tyranny and slavery out of the most extreme liberty." When many continue to call our government such, we should all be concerned.

When I wrote several times we are a Constitutional Federal Republic, how many realized it? As you say the Pledge of Allegiance to the Flag of the USA, do you say, "unto a Republic for which we stand?" If that is the case, why are so many calling our government a DEMOCRACY? They may appear similar, but there is a huge difference between the two.

Maybe that is why so many Americans don't go to the polls and vote in every election. There is no excuse for being ignorant about our government. In my lifetime, what I have learned so far about America's government, is a small percentage of what is taught in the classroom today. If this will not be taught in such educational institutions, it is up to us to learn everything ourselves. With the Internet available to most around the world, there is no excuse for being ignorant. There are libraries ready for us to learn things as well. Not everything online is factual, but that is no excuse for not connecting to websites that are giving out the facts. Helen Keller and Socrates both said, "The more you know, the more you do not know." Only by continual learning, we can know what is true and what is an outright lie. No one has ever said, "Ignorance is power."

Yes, through a hive mind, one can learn things far better than on the Internet alone, but no technology educates anyone directly. Even in ancient times of the lost civilizations of humanity, tools were used, but the learning process must be done by every student. The teacher/educator can do so much. The rest is completely up to each one of us.

The United States of America is a Constitutional Federal Republic. That means The Constitution is the highest authority of the Land. The next in charge is the Federal Government. Following that, State and local governments are all under a Rule of Law. Our Founding Fathers had a lot to say regarding a Republic vs a Democracy type government.

~~~~~

John Adams said, "Democracy, will soon degenerate into an anarchy, such an anarchy that every man will do what is right in his own eyes, and no man's life or property or reputation or liberty will be secure and every one of these will soon mold itself into a system of subordination of all the moral virtues, and intellectual abilities, all the powers of wealth, beauty, wit, and science, to the wanton pleasures, the capricious will, and the execrable cruelty of one or a very few."

Elbridge Gerry said, "The evils we experience flow from the excess of democracy. The people do not want virtue, but are the dupes of pretended patriots."

John Adams said, "Remember, democracy never lasts long. It soon wastes, exhausts, and murders itself. There is never a democracy that did not commit suicide."

Benjamin Rush said, "A simple democracy is the devil's own government."

~~~~~

What is a Democracy? It is simply what Thomas Jefferson said, "A Democracy is a mob rule of 51 to 49." There is no Life, Liberty, and Pursuit of Happiness with any mob-type government.

What is going on with abortion laws is just that — a demonic control of women and what they can do with their bodies. It isn't about prolife; instead is a direct violation of the First Amendment regarding Church and State. Bad leaders want to be written in the history books as tyrants. Good leaders simply do their jobs because they must be done.

This story is not a history lesson, but at the same time, good leaders with courage are not perfect living beings. Nearly every one of our Founding Fathers was a slave owner, but they created something that has not been fully replicated in human history. This story is to see how important it is to be a team player and continue going forward on that path through collective consciousness, if not a hive mind.

Good leaders are not doing their jobs for a reward. They do it because, at that moment, they just might be the only ones that can do what should have been done or the only ones that can achieve the right results. Whatever the reason, they don't do it to be put in history books. It is many years later someone writes about them after they are dead and gone. I am sure you read this quote before: "Buddha was not a Buddhist. Jesus was not a Christian. Muhammad was not a Muslim. They were teachers who taught Love... Love was their religion".

Sophia Vitaloti did not ask her father that question to get a standing ovation from the masses of people. It was later she realized she was only thinking of the whole of every living human being — both connected to their mental colloquium, the ones that were not connected, and the ones who may never take the plunge in doing so. What this 17-year-old teenager [soon to be a woman] needs is courage. She is already a natural leader. As a student clearly stated, she had helped many on campus.

Yes, there may be a huge difference in helping individuals when it is required, and there is a leadership role that will guide every living human being around the world through this class project which everyone will experience when it is completed. Sophia will not directly communicate with everyone, but it would not surprise me if she does with a few during her leadership of this project and years after.

****

As she was sitting in the passenger seat, she was quiet — too quiet.

Her mother while driving said, "There has been a great deal happening to you."

She did not say anything at first.

"Why not take a break? Even great artists, scientists, or whoever has to step away from it all for a short time."

It took a moment, but Sophia said without looking at her mother, "I know what I have done in helping other students on campus. I sort of accept why Autumn Heath has been attached to me — wait! No, I do not." She looked at her, "mom, how can I continue with this class project, most importantly, why has Ms. Miyu chosen me?"

She threw it back at her, "Who do you think should be in charge?"

Something hit her like a motivational lightning bolt. Feels like she does not want to do it; nevertheless, she realizes no one else could take her place. "If this is my duty after all, why am I feeling like I can't handle it?"

After turning right, she answered, "That is easy... more of an explanation; a lot has been put on you lately. You had a person that you thought was in your childhood dreams, and realizing you are growing up to be a very beautiful woman."

Sophia smiled, "Thanks, mom."

"Anytime, my daughter."

When they got home, she ended up sitting on her bed. She wanted to meditate on all that has happened to her. She needed to clear her mind to find her place in life. After ten minutes or so, she decided to check up on Autumn.

She replied, "I was waiting for you."

"Am I that special? I am no more or no less like anyone else."

"There is only one of us, Sophia. That makes you special in your own way."

"I hope I am not being rude, but that sounds so cliché."

"It does not have to be. That is completely up to you." She paused, "if I understand your mind right, I think you need to take your mother's advice — by taking it easy."

"I have thought about that, but if I am in charge, would it be right for me to step away?"

"Believe it or not, Sophia, taking a break from it for a few days will do more for everyone in this project. You have everyone working hard. If I see your mind right, you have someone that will help you do your part. Taking a break is not slacking off. I bet if you ask your classmates, they will tell you to rest up. You have already done a great deal. Let them do their part."

"Once I start something, I can't let go of it until I complete it."

"Let me make this suggestion, only act when it is necessary."

To change the subject, "How are you still using a child's voice."

"That is easy, my dear friend. My mind never fully developed as it could have. I have a sharp intellect, but I am far from..."

"I can tell you are more intelligent than I am. You have a maturity far beyond my expectations."

"This is difficult for me to explain. Yes, I have more intelligence than most because I worked harder than most. It is the physical that did not fully develop." She thought for a moment and asked, "have you learned about Doctor Stephen Hawking?"

"You mean the one with ALS or Amyotrophic Lateral Sclerosis?"

"That is him. Despite his whole body failing him, he continued to be a theoretical physicist, cosmologist, and author."

"HOLY COW! That is right." She paused, "are you telling me you were..."

"Not even close, but I did something that most refused to do."

"I don't think I am giving up. I just believe I am not fully capable."

"As your mother asked you, 'Who do you think should be in charge?' Think before answering."

She sighed, "I have no clue. After she asked me that, I felt like I could be the only one; nevertheless, I can't shake this impossible embrace."

"What do you feel?"

"When I first met Scarlet Knox, I thought she would fight me."

"Believe it or not, she is more of your advocate than you recently have learned."

"WHAT!? I need to talk to her. She is not connected, the last I have been told."

"Does she have to be?"

Sophia cleared her mind and concentrated on the moment. "If she is doing things on behalf of the class project... do I need to talk to her?"

"Don't change the subject. Whatever she is doing, she will talk to you directly or have someone at the school relay the information. I think what is overworking you is your emotions." She paused and continued, "it is also proof, only you can be in charge, but you can't do everything."

She cleared her mind once more, "I believe I overwork myself, time and time again, to cover up my fears."

"You can't fix everything or fix things before they are broken. For now, I suggest you moderate things. That is what every student wants you to do. They can do their part. Your suggestion that weekend was proof, to them, that you are in charge. Your instructor was not there. It was you, who went to Scarlet, that day. Zak did not suggest anything to you because he did not have to. You know what needs to be done. So far, you have done a wonderful job. Let every other student take the next move."

"Since I can't do anything at the moment. I will do as you suggest."

"Before I let you go to do that, answer my question."

"How do I feel? There is plenty of emotions going on in my head. I don't know if I can answer you."

"That is my point, dear friend. You don't need to be so emotional, to begin with."

As she opened her eyes, she saw Zak sitting in the same lotus position as she was barely a foot away from her. Seeing him on her bed with her, she smiled warmly. "Hello there. It is great to see you."

He gave a warm smile of his own. "I, too, meditate in my room after a full day in school. I see I was quieter since you woke up at your time than when I sat down."

"I was talking to Autumn Heath." She told him about the conversation.

He grinned, "I say, perfect timing. We all want you to lead us, but everyone wants me to tell you to slow down. A leader does not do the entire project. With ours, no one person can. Don't worry, you will have more to do, but everyone wants you to lead. We can do the rest."

"Like a General stays behind while her troops go to war?"

"It is true, we are not at war with the people who are not connected to our colloquium, hive mind, or whatever it should be called, but in a big way, the question you asked your father is a means to fight ignorance and get everyone — connected or not — to truly unite at we should have done at the beginning of civilization."

She thought about what her lover said. "If it is so difficult for humanity through the ages to connect as you are clearly saying, then it is worth going through the roadblocks, dark rain clouds, etc." She thought a bit longer, "if that is the case, is our hive mind system all that advanced if we have been doing the same thing as far back as the Neanderthals?" She paused, "you got me to believe we are not as connected as we may have believed. We need adversities to test our resolve. Without them, we can become comfortable. To grow, we must get our hands dirty and get into the middle of it."

Noda Miyu's voice came to them, "Exactly what Alexa was saying. What we call the hive is only a very complex relay system. Each human mind can store petabytes of information. What she told me after you all left, as if a third of the populace became too comfortable or technically, they got lazy on their responsibilities being a part of our colloquium, then it would be worse than never connecting to it, to begin with."

Zak said, "My love, the question you asked your father was what we all needed. Forget about the advanced technical aspect of it. I have understood that that is not what we should focus on anyhow. It is always the journey and never the destination."

Sophia broke their communication and went to her computer. She started to write...

~ ~ ~ ~ ~

If a collective consciousness is an evolution of communicating with the humanity through sharing of all the ideas and beliefs through the ages, then I wonder if we are doing it all wrong. Are we connected as we believe? I don't know if this class project can really answer these questions and fully get everyone to understand how important it is to communicate within the each other.

As we all know, the 21st century in America was bigger than a colossal failure in being a united nation, but we are alive today as the United States of America, but in a much different way. We have evolved from that dreadful roadkill, but we still have a great deal to learn. What have we all around the world really achieved through this advanced technology? Who are we if we still can't understand the basic principles of social intelligence? Is taking these baby steps what we should be doing, or should we be taking leaps now and then?

After telling Zak, 'Like a General stays behind while her troops go to war?' I wonder if I saw something that should be the core principle our class project should build upon. If I am right, it is like technology through artificial intelligence which allows us to achieve this hive mind technology is advancing while human beings are not. How have we advanced since everything nearly went up in ruins in the United States? I am wondering if we are still declining. The elements of what we have in this class project are simply a preamble. We need to get the ball rolling on what should be done.

~~~~~

Alexandra Rosa said, "If this does not prove to you that you are the only one that can lead this project, I assure you nothing will."

Ms. Miyu said, "There is no reason to send it to me. Yes, the entire class was monitoring you as you wrote it."

Yeva said, "Якщо ви цього не зрозумієте, я розіб'ю цю дупу, як ніколи раніше. Тут я? (Yakshcho vy ts'oho ne zrozumiyete, ya rozib'yu tsyu dupu, yak nikoly ranishe. Tut ya?) / If you
~~~~~

don't get it, I will bust that ass as I have never done before. Here me?"

Sophia laughed, "Так, це правда. Скільки разів ти мені так погрожував і нічого не зробив? (Tak, tse pravda. Skil'ky raziv ty meni tak pohrozhuvav i nichoho ne zrobyv?) / Yeah, right. How many times have you threatened me like that, and didn't do a damn thing?"

Because Zak could use the hive mental connection, he understood every word. He said, "You won't do that to Sophia, but I can and will."

Alexa said, "We are teasing you because we love you, girly. Yes, since Zak is your lover, he should be the one to help you help yourself."

Sophia made sure what she wrote was saved on her computer. The rest of the day, she spent time with her lover.

Living in a comfort zone as an individual or a nation of people is not progress at all. Technical advancements do not make a nation great. A collective consciousness or an advanced technical mental web of sharing the minds of billions is not progress, within itself. Humans can only evolve through a stoa if they participate in such an achievement.

This is no different from the people of the United States of America. A government of a Constitutional Federal Republic cannot function properly if there is a low voter turnout in every election. The corruption within the lawmakers will not yoke if they are allowed to rule freely. On the same train of thought, having billions of minds connected to a system where they can share ideas and values cannot succeed if individuals hide in the past of debauchery. Any structure cannot be built with insubstantial materials. A simple road cannot carry what is traveled if it is full of potholes and other calamities.

Sophia has nailed her concerns; it is not the ones that are not connected to their hive network, but the ones that are as still as the Dead Sea in Western Asia. If these billions of minds continue to be stagnant, the system that was designed to evolve humanity could destroy them and be put further back than anything recorded in Earth's history. They have been connected for many centuries now. It would be worse than genocide if they all did something worse than disconnect. They all must rejuvenate the core reason why they are connected, to begin with, or it could be the doom of humanity. It will be far more than medical reasons. That may have been the flint that started it all, but there is much more.

14

CHAPTER 13

After a few days of meeting Sophia at the park, on that first day, Scarlet Knox immediately realized what she asked her father, and it was not the words in themselves. Sophia was more concerned about the future of the human race than anything. Sometimes the right questions are asked in an offhand way to get the right results. Scarlet realized she had the hope of the human race in mind... of both who were connected and who was not.

At the same location there at the other day — at the State Park — she told them everything about Sophia and this project she was in charge of.

Madeine Rhodes, a dear friend of Scarlet at the age of 32 and an African-American, said, "WOW!! Just asking her father that question tells me she is serious about giving hope in this country and the world. What can we do to help?"

I think this class project needs to be online. I wrote an email to Sophia's instructor. After Noda Miyu replied, this will be a giant project. We need to raise the funds to put this online for all to read."

"Why does it need to be online at all? Could this school of hers do that?"

Scarlet said with certainty, "I thought of that, but for this to reach everyone around the world, it must be available for everyone." She paused, "I saw how concerned she was about helping everyone."

Hazel Webb, another dear friend of Scarlet at the age of 37 who was born in Australia but lived in the United States at the age of four, said, "What makes you think that? You only spoke with her for a very short time. I think you need to talk with her more."

She smiled, "Trust me, everyone, I would not have gathered you all here if it was not this serious."

Madeine said, "When you talked to me through our smartphones the other day, you gave me a lot of information. I have to admit you have convinced me, but you have to give us more to raise this kind of money to allow the world to see this project once it is completed."

"That is why we all are here. I am not asking any of you five to connect your mind to this system, but Sophia Vitaloti has made me think of doing it. Before I do, I want to see this class project, that she is in charge of, be put online for all to learn from. It would not hurt for us to do our own since we are not connected."

Guy Leon, born and raised in the United States at the age of 36, said, "Since this project is new, we should take this slow. What you told me over the phone, I would believe this young woman has a lot on her."

"That is why we are here; we need to help her. Yes, she will be in charge of the project, and I believe the only one, but she is young and only one person. She will not be able to do this alone no matter how intelligent she has already shown me the other day. I was also told by her Sociology instructor, she was the one to have them all meet in this part not that far from where we were then."

Jeremy Logan blurted out, "HOLY COW! I now understand what you saw in her that day."

Madeine said, "I think the first thing we need to do is find out more about this project before we go fundraising."

Scarlet replied, "Read about the news reporters at her home that day. Read or hear it from her on what she told them all." She paused, "what has concerned me is not for the ones that have not been connected, but the ones that have been. From what I have gathered, it appears they are mind-numbed over it. I mean I think that is what is concerning Sophia the more. It is not who has not been connected, but the ones who have and are living as they are not."

Guy replied, "I see why you are serious about us being here. I wonder if we need to be connected to help everyone, especially this 17-year-old woman. Yes, she would be called a girl at her age, but she appears to be more mature than everyone here.

Scarlet said with all the determination in her voice, "That is why she needs all the help she can. This project might be the lifeline experience for the entire human race, especially for the ones that have been connected nearly all their lives."

Madeine was amazed at what she said, "I, for, one believe you." She gave a warm smile, "believe it or not, I believed you already, but what you just said... WOW!"

"I believe Sophia to be a big wow." She paused, "it is up to you all if you want to be connected yourself, but it is not necessary to help her."

Jeremy said, "Nothing can help her by what we do with our personal lives. All we can do is support her."

Scarlet said, "That is why I want to have this report of theirs online. As more learn from it, more will help out too."

He said, "Slow down. Let her make the next move."

Madeine replied, "She has... more moves that I have seen from sociology. I believe what Sophia has started and wants to achieve is far beyond what any specialists can achieve."

Scarlet gave a big smile, "That is what I saw in her the first time we met in this park. She can be a great leader one day. Ms. Noda Miyu did not have to assign her to this project..."

Everyone interrupted her, "She did it herself!"

Scarlet gave a bigger smile, "EXACTLY!"

Jeremy asked, "How long will it take to finish this class project?"

"I believe it will be ongoing. You heard her at the news conference the other day. It is still all over social media. This project is already online and strong. The students of this sociology class will present is the results of what Sophia will learn herself. All we will do is help provide the means to put that information to everyone else."

Hazel said, "I believe we need to meet up with her or her classmates. We could help with something. If this is as serious as you are saying, this may be too big for her, if not the entire class."

"That is why we are here, to begin with. I simply wanted us ready when they do need us."

"That puts a huge spin on what we said here in this park the other day... the day you met Sophia; nevertheless, I am believing what we need to do is change our perspective." Hazel paused, "think about it; it is not Sophia that needs to grow up, but us — mentally anyhow."

Jeremy said, "If I understand why these students are doing this class project, I think it is the whole of the planet. While studying the early 21st century in America, a lot of people fell too deep into their comfort zones. Why for many decades they had a low voter turnout in the free world. Even to this day, there is still talk of a Blue or Red Wave. Forget the politics... even with this class project. Billions of minds may be already connected to this hive network, stoa, colloquium, or whatever we should call it. What good is all of it if we are not serious about living in it?"

Scarlet said, "So you believe we need to get more dynamic than providing a website or whatever?"

"INDEED, I AM! If we don't get involved this way, what good is this class project once completed? I think we need to allow the masses to meet what Sophia Vitaloti started by asking her father her question. These students can deal with this project. It will be easy to have this project online for all to experience. If we don't get most if not everyone involved, what these students can do will be useless."

"After hearing you, my friend, I have to agree. By your description of her, it would not surprise me if Sophia could do this very thing without half realizing what she had done."

Guy replied in amazement, "HOLY COW! Are you telling me, she is that influential?"

Scarlet gave a big smile, "Would we all be here in this park again so soon if she did not influence me that day? Yes, Guy, she is beyond that. She has a gift that could achieve her goal with or without this class project."

****

Days after Alexandra Rosa was talking to the students for the first time, Scarlet and each of her friends freely decided to be connected to this colloquium or hive mind network. She gave word to Sophia's mother that she wanted to talk to her daughter at the park to tell her all they had in mind. Scarlet did not tell Pippa she was connected. She wanted to tell Scarlet that personally.

When she was a good distance from her, she did not have to use her hive-mind abilities to see Sophia was mentally exhausted. "Talking about perfect timing. This connection does have some great advantages, but I believe she has overworked herself. That may be why Pippa was eager for me to be with her daughter."

As Scarlet was walking closer to the table she was sitting at, she grinned warmly inwardly. "Yep, I was right... perfect timing." After arriving at earshot, "I see you need my help more than you believe."

Sophia looked up with a smile, "This project is growing faster than an atomic bomb, but physics is not one of my strong points." She quietly looked at her for a mere second, but to her, it was much longer. Before Scarlet had the chance to sit down, Sophia gave a big ear-to-ear smile, "YOU ARE CONNECTED!"

After sitting, she said, "Yes, I am. We all are."

"SAY WHAT!? You mean all that was with you that day?"

She told her everything in their recent meeting.

Sophia nearly went back to her slumped posture and said, "That is what I am doing... or I should say this project is growing the more we work on it. If you can convince the world..."

"Have you not read what everyone is saying on the many social media platforms?"

"I have and I wonder if it will be enough."

"I think what is exploding... or better yet imploding... is the confidence in yourself. Trust me, girl, you can do this because you have done a great deal already. Your instructor, Noda Miyu, keeps me abreast of all you and your class have done." She paused, "believe it or not, you have done more than advanced classes in college. I wished I had you on my team when I was there a few years back." She paused again, "that is not important right now. You are. What I have learned from Ms. Miyu, and what was running through your head just now, I think it is our time to add our contribution."

Sophia smiled, "Thanks, and yes, I do."

She studied her for a moment, "You are still bothered by it. Know you can talk to me."

"I knew that before I walked to meet you on that first day."

"WOW! You are intelligent."

"Yes and no. Nearly at birth, I realized I had a strong empathic ability. I am known to be wrong about things..."

"Don't worry, sweetie. No one is perfect. I didn't get instant anything when I first connected to this hive-mind system. I am sure you did not either. Your abilities came from you." Scarlet paused, "what you need to do is rest. With me and my dearest friends helping, this project will end up doing great. Studying you as I was walking closer, I think you would do a hundred times more if you have every single person on this planet doing their part. If you and this project are still being talked about on social media, then in their way, they are doing that."

"I think that is why I can go on and do more, but you are right, I am exhausted."

"Why not get involved on these social media platforms? Without asking everyone to take part in this class project of yours, I am sure thousands will type their replies. They may be waiting for you to get online and simply communicate with them."

All of a sudden Noda Miyu appeared. She said, "□□□□□□□□ (derukui wa utareru) / The nail that sticks out is struck." She paused and continued in English, "this means they are already ready to work together for the greater good of all who are connected."

Sophia said, "HOLY COW!"

Scarlet smiled, "I am not surprised about this at all."

Sophia asked her instructor, "□□□□□□□□□□□□□□ □□□□□□□□□□□□□□□□ (Karera wa ima junbi ga dekite imasu ka? Kore wa omottayori mo hayaku susunde imasu) / Are they ready, now? This is going faster than I thought."

Scarlet answered, "□□□□□□□□□ □□ (Chūi shite imasen ka? Watashi wa, sōsharumedia dakedenaku, onrain de kore hodo ninki ga aru koto o shirimasendeshita. Sore wa subete anata to kankei ga arimasu.) / Have you not been paying attention? I have known nothing to be so popular online less alone social media, and it has everything to do with you."

Sophia smiled, "GREAT! You can speak Japanese, and very accurately if I may say."

"I have been doing so nearly all my life. My mother was Japanese. She died several years back."

Ms. Noda Miyu said, "You should stop sulking and get in touch with everyone online. Allow the rest of the class to do this project. You got that ball rolling. It is your duty to connect with everyone else who wants to participate as well."

With a surprised look "HOLY COW! Everyone?"

Both Noda Miyu and Scarlet said, "YES, everyone."

Still amazed, "How can I make such a difference in a short time? There has to be more to this."

Noda Miyu said, "You did not do this all by yourself. You gave us all your heart and love for humanity being connected to our colloquium."

Scarlet continued, "You also did this for all who were not."

Sophia said, "□□□□□□□□□□ (i no naka no kawazu taikai wo shirazu) / A frog in a well knows nothing of the sea."

Scarlet gave a big smile, "Yes, my dear friend. You are that sea."

Noda Miyu clearly said, "She is much more. She is the ocean."

Now Sophia completely understood this is her duty. It was why she joined this colloquium in the first place. She may not have realized it then, but she does now. The moment she connected, it became her duty to allow everyone to be connected from within their souls to themselves and everyone else around the globe.

When Sophia got home, she immediately went to her computer to read what people had been saying on all the social media platforms. "What do I say? How do I start the conversation?"

Scarlet said to her through the hive mind, "Before you do that, my dear friend, you need to create a good username for yourself."

"I usually don't log in... well I did years ago, but..."

"That does not matter."

"OH BOY! I am nervous."

"Yes, you are, but that is normal. In the past, you helped a few at a time. Use those skills and memories to do so here."

After calming herself a bit, she asked, "What is a good username?"

All of a sudden an image of a word came to her, and it felt like it was from everyone that was connected to the hive mind... Bodhi.

Sophia said out loud, "What does that mean?"

After she opened her eyes, her answer was given, "It means, Sanskrit for "enlightenment" or "awakening.""

She blurted out, "OH! MY! GOD! This is my duty!"

Before she had the chance to create a new account, she realized it was already done for her. At the top left of the browser screen, she saw a message, Welcome, बोधि (Bodhi).

Still a bit nervous, she typed in, "Hello everyone."

Yeva replied, "Hello, Bodhi. The whole class has been talking a great deal. The world is ready to help."

Tears of joy ran down her face, "OH, MY GOODNESS. I don't believe it!"

In moments, under twenty replied, "It is our honor for what you started for every one of us. Bodhi, you are our awakening. What more should we do?"

Sophia started to cry for joy more. With her hands over her face, barely seeing through her fingers. They gave her a moment to reply. She typed, "Thanks all. I now know it is my duty to guide you to what started long before I was born."

Someone wrote, "That is why you are our Bodhi. It was you that enlightened us all."

Another person wrote, "I can't say how many, but from what I have learned, more have connected because of you. What you shared with us at the news conference the other day, at least those people have stopped fearing being connected."

A third person wrote, "For the ones that have been already, we are ready to do our part in what you have started."

Sophia wrote, "I am learning a great deal about the history of our colloquium, but far from what I need to learn."

That same third person replied to it, "We all are, thanks to you. This is your duty and class project, but you will never be alone after what has expired... from you."

After looking at the clock on her computer, she cursed. She typed in, "I need to get ready for bed if I can sleep at all after what I have experienced from all of you."

Yeva said, "We all will guide you, girly. See you in the morning."

Sophia logged out, turned off her computer, and got ready for bed.

15

CHAPTER 14

Sophia slept in because it was still the weekend... Saturday to be precise. Do not get confused. Yes, most if not all around the world understand that time is much more than linear, but they all still use the same day by day, month by month, and year by year system. To be honest, old the Gregorian calendar has been forgotten. If you study ancient history, humanity went by an interminable types of calendars throughout their history. I would not doubt it there is more... even the Neanderthals. Because there is not recorded records, it does not mean it did not happen. Scientists have recently realized, early mankind was more intelligent than first understood.

Believe it or not, human nature mostly stays the same. We have our struggles and in time overcome them. We have wars and rumors of wars throughout time. Sophia — as she is now known as Bodhi. Yes, that name is a boy's name of Sanskrit origin, but for our protagonist it is synonymous with the concept of nirvana and the final goal of Buddhism. Sophia, actually means, in the Greek, wisdom. As she fulfills the name Bodhi, her wisdom and she she shares will do more for humanity. She was the world's enlightenment to a better tomorrow. In time, she will lead the world on what their colloquium mind in a whole new journey.

Believe it or not, we are meant to solve our own problems. This hive mind was never to abolish any responsibility of their own lives. Any advancements we achieve is learning to think as individuals while working as one — no matter the size of the team. The reason why the military is so arduous; to be bluntly honest, most individuals don't know how to think at all. They can barely administer themselves. Most depend too much on others... in literally everything — including thinking. Most define hive mind as being controlled by a queen or some central individual. When politics, religious leaders, or whomever are corrupt, their followers are mind manipulated. Dictators thrived on such maneuvering manipulations, but their followers can easily break free in any given moment — like the story of the Devil Tarot card.

Subconsciously, Sophia realized the dangers... not being manipulated in this manner, but the softness of their brains... their general way of life was divagating. Their lazy mental attitude did not degrade overnight; instead, their minds lost the eye of the tiger. When you go down the wrong journey of life, it gets harder and harder to go back the way you originated. It is no difference when getting lost. When the mind is lost, there is no truths to guide. Fundamentalism sets in. Eventually it causes legalism (of adherence to precise laws) without any discipline at all other these so-called leaders leading the blind. In another word, false truths that is incoherent to reality. Good leaders do not need deceitfulness to enlighten others. The strong drive for a team to achieve on their own allows progress to advance. That means, advancements are for the mature mind in a given team, group, society, or nation.

Sophia finally got out of bed to have her morning shower. By the time she was done, her mother had breakfast ready.

"Good morning, mom."

"Good morning, Bodhi.

She nearly collapsed in the kitchen.

"None of that."

"OH, MY! I was hoping that was a dream. I was half asleep when I first corresponded with all of them."

Pippa nearly grinned, "Nearly the whole colloquium is calling you that."

"OH, MY GOD!" She quickly sat in spare chair of the dinning room if they had guests over. It was simply out of the way between the kitchen and the dinning room. Sophia continued, "this can't be real."

Her father deliberately spoke in Greek to get her to concentrate, "Τι περιμένατε από όλα όσα έχετε κάνει (Ti periménate apó óla ósa échete kánei) / What did you expect on all you have done."

She felt like she wanted to hide in a dark hole, "Το μόνο που έκανα ήταν μια ερώτηση. Πώς μπορεί το σύνολο των πλατφορμών μέσων κοινωνικής δικτύωσης και ολόκληρο το συνέδριο να μου δώσει ένα τέτοιο όνομα. (To móno pou ékana ítan mia erótisi. Pós boreí to sýnolo ton platformón méson koinonikís diktýosis kai olókliro to synédrio na mou dósei éna tétoio óno-ma.) / All I asked was a question. How can the whole of social media platforms and the entire colloquium give me such a name."

He answered in English with that Greek accent, "Philosophy of science without history of science is empty; history of science without philosophy of science is blind," He paused, "you are blinding yourself of what you have done. You are a natural philosopher. That is why you could ask the question. Because you are young, does not mean you are wrong. That is why Noda Miyu gave you the class assignment. It grew because of the heart that is in you. Since you did so in the respect of all of humanity, everyone wants to help you fulfill it. You alone can't complete it, but you gave the loving spark that flamed it."

She did not know how, but she new her Bampás was right on the money.

Sophia's mother suggested, "After you eat breakfast, why not talk to more. You could have done so last night." After bringing more to the table, she continued, "the more you correspond with more and more, you will see how much they want to help you. This is your journey, my daughter, but as General Patton once said, 'Individuality is a bunch of horse crap.' You will need others."

Nikolas said, "That is why you are overwhelmed. You want to do it all yourself. Allow everyone that is willing to help you — to do their portion of your journey. It is why we have cars; there is no way we can walk all the way from point A to point B."

Her mother smiled, "You will make it. We all have faith in you."

After eating breakfast and helped clean up the dishes, she went to her room to do just that.

Yeva wrote, "It is about time you logged in. Why in the hell did you log off so quickly. Your excuse was..."

"Shut up, you."

"You know I can't do that."

She laughed out loud before typing a response, "OH, I know." She paused, "how is the project going."

Abigail Perry was quietly reading what they were saying, "Bodhi, you are not supposed to be concerned about that."

"HELL! I am apart of this project as everyone else."

"We know that." Abigail paused, "before I tell you, I want you to promise that you will not be overly concerned..."

She interrupted, "I will promise nothing. Even my mom said I should go online and talk to you all more. If I am accurate, that is my way to advise."

A person, by the username of, cyborg505 said, "Bodhi, your mother was correct, but we can feel your mind is overstimulated by it."

"Yes, I am. How can my question I asked my Bampás have caused so much from everyone?"

Cyborg505 said, "It allowed us to rethink our lives as we are connected to the hive mind. I can't know how many, but a great deal have joined because of you."

Sophia had water works going down her cheeks.

Many have replied to the same thing... including the ones just blended.

After crying for joy once again, Sophia came to realize her duty. She closed her eyes and put herself into the core of the hive network. She immediately felt peace. It was like she could not be anywhere else. She was not just Sophia or Bodhi... but both. She was the Wisdom of the final Enlightenment that will transgress the existence of everyone to a better place. Sophia Bodhi could feel the minds of all on Earth and everyone of them were waiting to be led to Nirvāṇa.

It appeared to Sophia an immeasurable time before she opened her eyes — not to break away from this wonderful experience. She felt something that her soul needed to be — Zak Harris — which was right there in her bedroom.

****

During the weekend, Sophia had the opportunity to flex her mind within her new skills with the colloquium — Zak made sure of it. Yes, he wanted to spend time with her romantically, but this was her duty.

As Pippa was driving, Sophia said, "It is like I was made to do what I can with our hive mind system. How? Was my mind in this system before I was born?" "lately, it sure feels that way. I feel that I am connected to Autumn Heath, or why she could find me when I was a young girl."

After she started to drive from a street light, she answered, "Does finding this information make a difference."

She had a good question. She thought for a moment, "When I asked Bampás that question, I did not expect this. I think I need to know why this is happening."

She smiled, "Have you figured out why you asked him. Sometimes we go around the Maypole in a continuous circle to find the answers to life..."

"You are thinking, the center."

"Yes, I am."

"OH, MY GOD. I can read minds!"

"What is so wrong with that?"

"I do not want to violate anyone's privacy. They have their right..."

"Yes, they do. You are again not centering yourself. You can't doubt yourself any longer. Your new skills and abilities will only frighten you. As Luke 12:48 says, 'From everyone to whom much has been given, much will be required; and to whom they entrusted much, of him they will ask all the more.'"

Sophia sighed, "I know; I think that is what concerns me." She paused, "nevertheless, I feel... I don't know... like I am home. If

Zak was not in my bedroom the other day, I would have staid in that mental matrix. I had the hardest time breaking from it this morning."

"As far as you know, you could still be where you say."

Sophia broke out of it. "OH, MY GOD! I am late for school. This is getting dangerous." "this is weird, mom would have snapped me to reality. She usually does that."

Scarlet Knox said, "Nonsense! Have you not forgotten, you were sequestered from school from... for the time being."

She got worried, "I can't stop my whole life."

"No one wants to do that."

She calmed her mind to reality, "How can I be with mom driving a moment ago? It was so real."

"As you mentioned a mental matrix, you can put yourself in a visual aspect of reality. Trust me, no one else can do that." She paused, "think of it as day dreaming, but you created this virtual world being with your mother as she was driving."

"I hope I can know the difference."

"You will, my friend. It could be why you broke from what you created in your mind."

She had a thought. "We need to talk. Let me see if I can put both of us in that park." Before any one of them could realize it, they were there. Sophia said, "It feels so real."

"Yes, it does. You are more intelligent than you let on."

They sat at the near by picnic table.

Sophia said, "This feels more than real. What is going on?"

She smiled out of her enthusiasm, "It was you that created this virtual world. You tell me."

After studying her surrounding, "That was right, it was raining. In fact it was supposed to rain all week."

Suddenly they smelt something.

Scarlet said, "I adore the smell after a rainstorm."

She giggled, "This can't be real."

"In actuality, it is not , but it is your virtual representation of your own experiences."

"WOW!! I wonder what more I can do?" She was about to forget why she sent them to this park, "somehow I need you. I mean, you were there... at the real park. You know knew what I was thinking."

"It was more like what you were feeling. We all can do that. If what you described about that monk helping you, he knew too."

"He did not give me instruction as such..."

"Love, no one can give you advice other than yourself especially when you are so intelligent. Your monk only gave you what you needed to know."

She thought it over. "You are right! Wow!"

"You are a big wow, Sophia Bodhi."

She half smiled, "Thanks."

"I think your problem is having more faith in yourself. It is true, you can't do everything, but you have at least given convenience in everyone including me."

"I knew I could talk to you."

She looked serious, "You can always talk to me, sweetie. For what you have done for me and my friends, we will always be their for you."

Sophia gave a warm smile, "Thanks. I will need it."

"Don't think you are alone. You have Zak, Yeva, Somova, and all your friends." She gave a big grin, "you have everyone on the grid. Just give yourself the credit you deserve." She paused, "we all do."

"WOW! What a life. I never thought this would could happen when I first connected." She sat up straight and seriously said, "I don't know how I will do it, but I know it is my duty."

The whole sociology class said, "YES, IT IS!"

Noda Miyu said, "□□□□□□□□□□□□□□□□□□□□□□□□ (Anata-nara kitto seikō shimasu, Sofia bodi.) / You will make it, Sophia Bodhi."

Yeva said, "It should be the other way around because she is full of..."

Sophia teased, "Shut up, you."

Everyone laughed.

Scarlet said, "Now, I know you will make it, I will leave it to you to practice on what you are meant to do. Remember, love, you can talk to me anytime." She vanished.

For the remaining of the day, Sophia did just that.

* * * * * * * * * *

The next morning while eating breakfast, Sophia asked her mother, "Did you realized our conversation, or did I make the whole thing up."

She smiled warmly, "As I told you, where would I be other than your mind, baby, so yes, you and I corresponded even though it was in what you called, a matrix of your mind.

She sighed in relief, "Good, I thought I was in that movie with Keanu Reeves many years ago."

Sensing what was in her mind that something was troubling her, Pippa kept silent. She had to talk it out herself.

Even thought I have seen a few of the old movies, including that one. I sort of enjoyed them."

"You know you can always watch them in the archives." Pippa realized that was not what was concerning her.

"I would like to know more about how we connected in the first place. It has to be more than Autumn Heath."

"Baby, listen to me." When Sophia heard her say that, it was essential, "learning from history is paramount, while at the same time, you will learn nothing."

Her father came in to eat breakfast himself, "You have not learned why I said, 'Philosophy of science without history of science is empty; history of science without philosophy of science is blind.' Until you do, then you may never learn why your question was so vitally important. Academic knowledge will not help you learn your life alone if at all. Don't get me wrong, it has its importance, but you are sequestered not to be in school for that same reason."

"What is that, Bampás?"

"That is easy and hard. The easy part, this is your duty to guide the billions of minds out of the rut you saw them before you were connected."

"OH, MY!! I did so to save them."

"EXACTLY!! You know need to use this matrix — NO! It has nothing to do with that movie at all. You are only allowing that to help you figure out things out."

"You mean to tell me our experiences make up reality?"

"To where it counts, yes. We are breathing the same air and experiencing life all around, but when it comes to our personal lives, our brains interprets reality, so in all right, reality it an illusion."

Sophia as in a trance said, "Our Colloquium is another reality. It is like the evolution of humanity. We are not evolving enough or at least as we should."

Noda Miyu out of nowhere said and everyone at the dinner table heard her, "Yes, Sophia Bodhi. That is why I changed my class curriculum around it. I realized the fullness of why you asked your father that question. Don't be blinded by that academics of the origin of our Colloquium. If you could learn it all, I doubt it will help you fulfill your duty."

Why did Autumn Heath contact me?"

Alexandra Rosa said, "That is simple. Your mind is a wonder that supersedes a great deal. I believe now, it was you that healed her from her disease."

"WHAT!? How! It was endless years before I was born." She realized the question she asked her mother, "so my mind was in this matrix before I was born?"

Pippa answered, "No one can know. As in Christianity, there is a spiritual life and a biological life. There are many detonations still that believe in reincarnation. I can't say if that is real or not, but it could be your spiritual life always existed."

Alexa in which she refers to be called than Alexandra said, "I believe it is academic and stories, parables, or whatever one should call them to explain the unexplainable."

Sophia thought for a moment, "I doubt that Autumn would know, but I remember vividly we corresponded when I was young — even before I was connected."

Noda Miyu said, "What you need to focus on is the here and now. Discover your answer to your question while in the hive mind system. It is you that wanted to help everyone, so get to know everyone. Know the playing field of this new evolution."

16

CHAPTER 15

Sophia Bodhi was able to stretch her mind to the whole world through the hind mind network. Since she was dedicated to preserve personal freedoms, she wanted everyone to know she would never take the liberties they had in this system.

She could not know how many, but they replied to her in their different ways, what she had been doing was not that at all. Each mind realized they had to better themselves — for themselves and the whole of humanity. They reassured her they did not considered her a savior like any religion, but they will show her the utmost respect and love.

She immediately realized what she had done so far — it was not the question she asked her father, but the deep embedded reason she asked it. As her father had said, "Philosophy of science without history of science is empty; history of science without philosophy of science is blind." It was Immanuel Kant (April 22, 1724 - February 12, 1804) that said that. He meant that science and philosophy should be one. That means as far as the fastness of the hive mind, everyone should work together. That was what Sophia Bodhi realized without knowing the details before she connected to the hive mind herself.

As the United States has caused a ripples of corruption and derogation of the Rule of Law (which means a Republic), far too many to count on how those corrupt politicians have tried to destroy something that had never been created in human history — a Constitutional Federal Republic that was ratified in 1788. She did not know if what the Founding Fathers had created died before their hive mind existed, but since she was born, she knew it existed in her heart, and she wanted the WE THE PEOPLE of this wonderful world full of human beings connected to this vast mental hive to have the grand opportunity to evolve from that same Republic. The government of today is more than what it had been around the world. Everything was centered on this extremely and complex mental connection.

"How can I do all that is required without destroying the many, many cultures of endless nations?"

Another mind said, "Sophia Bodhi, we know you will not do any harm to us."

"Thank you. I know I won't directly do that, but how can I guide you to this Nirvāṇa without complications."

"That is life, but these complications you speak will never be done by you."

"How do you know that?"

"By the mind you have shared with us." The individual paused, "the concerns you have in what your nation failed to do in the early 21st century, was not done by you. Every nation around the world had dealt with corruption of one type or the other. As you can see in every individual mind, those nation survived. Yes, they did so by a thin thread, but that is a metaphor. I mean, the people that removed those politicians and elected better leaders were much stronger than the corruption itself. This took many years. What was done wasn't done overnight. When we all make mistakes and learn from them, we learn so much more than in a calm academic classroom experience."

She smiled warmly in her mind, "You are a wise person."

"It is just the simple truth... no more, no less. Know this if any-thing, you can't do this alone, and every mind will help you fulfill your duty."

After several hours being immersed into the depths of the collo-quium — as Alexandra Rosa called it, Sophia said out loud, "What do I call it? It feels like a epistemological meaning then a collective." "Yes, I philosophical word. This is more then a mere name. This is something that was meant to happen. Something that we should have been the day we were born."

Autumn Heath said, "I believe that very thing. I also believe this system that has allowed you all to collect yourselves mentally, should have a better name."

"I feel that I was the one that saved you from your Rett Syndrome, but how?"

She said cheerfully, "You were. That is how you know me. It is your mind created this system."

"If you say so, but just the same, I believe what you are saying. I am confused on how I could do that."

"You told me that time had no boundaries." "It is a lot more than mere time and how you are measuring it."

"I don't understand. Are you telling me, I went in the past from some unknown future?"

"Not you... entirely. Think of it as the matrix of what created the spark of what you call the colloquium mind." I sense you are grasping it all, but because you are measuring time as linear, you can't fully grasp what I could be telling you."

"That is why I don't like that name. What we have now is more than an academic conference or whatever. What I have been experiencing for nearly a week is so much more than a mere gathering." A word came to her mind, "Esotericism."

Autumn said, "That word is a Western form of spirituality that stresses the importance of the individual effort to gain spiritual knowledge. Are you implying our hive mind system has risen to something spiritual." "Oh, wow! How much I want to tell you all of it. If I did, you would get more confused. Why you can bring your mind into a different reality, it is how you think. It is why you were chosen." She paused, "it was you that had your mother state that Bible verse through your own thoughts."

"I know; we talked about that when she got home. I know the Christian Bible and its doctrines, but that does not mean I want..."

"Sweetie, that is not what I asked."

She gave a long pause, "I don't know why that word popped in my head. Because of Bam... no, daddy, is a philosopher, I know good many sects of that era."

"What are you looking for? I mean what is so wrong in calling it a hive mind, colloquium, or a stoa?"

"Those words sounds to cold. After experiencing the network, and I have not experienced half of it, I saw those minds deserve something better. Thinking about it, I don't think esotericism is enough." She paused in thought, "I remember, esoteric means the quality of having an inner or secret meaning. I need to find a word that will fit everyone in this hive."

It was like every mind said at once, "Esosophia!"

Sophia was happy she was sitting as she was talking with Autumn in her mind. She would not have handled it. She practically cried her eyes out.

Somova said, "Bodhi Sophia, you are the one that is leading us. Your question that you asked your daddy had caused us to wake up from our comfort zones. Our minds are not just connected to nanobots. It was you that saved Autumn Heath's life. I don't know how, but if you did not save her life, we would not be in this esosophia — within wisdom — today."

Sophia cried the more for pure joy.

"Get to know yourself and this esosophia. You may learn everything and a bit more, but never rush into it."

"If I was in the matrix while Autumn was a live, then that may prove reincarnation is real, but if that is so, would I have not forgotten?"

"Do you remember it?"

"No, that is my point."

"You may never learn any more about that era. If you find anything about it, then it will be what you were meant to know in this life time."

"It was like a dream in knowing her."

"What I get from your mind, it is barely bits and pieces." "It is why I am talking to you. It was Autumn that got me to talk to you. Why I did so quickly, I knew you. All she had to say, Sophia was stressed out."

"I knew her name... like we were great friends."

"That is all you need to know for you two to live in the now."

Sophia changed the subject by asking, "Why 'eso-?'"

"Everyone is within your enlightenment. Why else has it been called nearly since the beginning." "Trust me, my friend, we all realized you were a very special individual. How much you have helped students with there classwork... and nearly before they had the chance to ask. Your mannerisms as far as I have known you, was a dead giveaway. I was not surprised that you are the one that help build this mental system if not the only one that could do it."

"WHAT!? Alex called it a colloquium that day in school."

"I thought you would have figured it out that an academic conference would not fit. We all did."

"I should have." She paused, "it may be why I didn't like it."

Autumn said, "How do you like the name... I called it."

"OH! MY! I remember."

Somova said, "Only bits and pieces. I see it in your mind, and I know you, girlfriend." "What I am sensing in Autumn's mind, you two are the same person. No wonder she could call on me to help. Yes, you have a life before this one. I would love to talk to her about it more."

Autumn said, "After you cured me and stopped communicating with me, I wanted the name of this mental matrix to have your name. Since your name means, wisdom, it was proper to call it, esosophia — within wisdom."

"Why did I leave you. That does not sound wise."

Her Russian friend answered, "You always know when to leave quietly and peacefully when the job is done. It is in your nature to allow others to live out their own lives once your work was complete and not before."

****

When Sophia broke from the the adventuring in the mental matrix. She realized it was nightfall, but she realized she had to write something down with what she recently experienced. She stood up from her bed from meditating and went to her computer.

~~~~~

I feel what is going on is more than just helping Autumn. She stated, my mind created the system. I have to believe my devotion for helping others allowed me to do so, but this is something extra-ordinary. How could this come into existence? Is all that Autumn recently told me a allegory?

When she first told me this, I was disoriented and liberated over it. I have no knowledge of medicine especially of those medical less alone technical advancements. I went through mom's library, and I could not find anything. I was hoping to find some medical or technical journals about it. Either this existed or it did not. I could not get anything on who helped. I mean, I was told friends and family of Autumn's connected to this system just for her.

This is a convoluted time paradox. Autumn was born long before I was. I somehow believe all she told me, but how? Was I this Sophia Bodhi before they gave me this title? There are too many questions and no answers, and it appears to me, the questions are multiplying.

I think the new name... wait a minute! It was named, esosophia before I was born — some time after I cured Autumn. She admitted to that. I need to know more what occurred that day... or how long it was when I was with her. I don't know. I am so befuddled. How it feels, we never departed. She contacted me some time after I cured her — I guess. This time thing is weird. It was like we were dear friends for years. If that monk is right, I have already fulfilled my duty, and I am doing it again — by curing every mind in this esosophia.

~~~~~

Ms. Noda Miyu said, "□□□□□□□□□□□□□(Konbanwa, Sofia bodidesu.) / Good evening, Sophia Bodhi."

She smiled, "□□□□□□□□□□□ □□□□□□□□□□□□□□□ □□□□□□□□□□□□□□□□ (Noda Miyū-san, konbanwa. Anata to hanasete totemo ureshīdesu. Anata no jugyō o kesseki shite shimaimashita.) / Good evening Ms. Noda Miyu. It is great to be talking with you. I have missed your classes."

[They continued to communicate in American English]

"None of that, Bodhi."

"I know my duty... more than ever."

"That is why I am talking to you, Sophia. Who would not want their lives back in the vastness of what you have been doing since day one."

"How could I helped Autumn?"

"The how, why, or whatever sparked your question to your father won't give you the answers within itself. You have to follow your heart. It appears you had done that with Autumn Heath in saving her life if not all the souls connected to this esosophia."

Feeling a bit apprehensive having everyone know what has recently occurred.

"Sophia Vitaloti! You know better than to feel that way." She paused, "but it is understandable. To be honest, I would feel the same way."

"□□□□□□ □□□□□□□□□□ (Arigatō. Sore wa arigataidesu.) / Thank you. I appreciate it."

"□□□□□□ (Dai kangeidesu.) / You are most welcome." She paused, "I think you have a good grip on the situation. I am impressed how well you speak Japanese. Especially at your age."

"What now?"

"Get some sleep. I will add what you just wrote to the class project."

"Thanks. I didn't write it for that. In all that I recently experienced, I had to write something. I could have written more, but like you said, I need to get to bed."

Before Sophia Bodhi could do or think any thing more, once she hit the pillow, she was out cold in slumber.

****

The next morning, Sophia realized she slept in her clothes. It is something she usually does not do. She smelled her left arm pit. "I can see why I don't. Time for a shower."

After putting her smelly clothes in the hamper in her walk in closet, she took off too the room across the hall — the bathroom.

It took her a few moments to get completely cleaned, and moments she was dressed. "Perfect timing. I smell breakfast. It smells like mom's has cooked a feast." She finally realized it. "Zak was there. I must have zonked out when he arrived."

Zak said, "Actually, it was when you were writing that recent paper for the class project."

"How!? It was not much."

"Apparently you were exhausted. You wrote several pages."

"WHAT!?" She immediately turned on her computer and loaded up the file. "OH! MY! I remember."

"You thought it was the first four paragraphs?"

"Yes, I did." She stared at the screen and read it all.

~~~~~

I feel what is going on is more than just helping Autumn. She stated, my mind created the system. I have to believe my devotion for helping others allowed me to do so, but this is something extra-
~~~~~

ordinary. How could this come into existence? Is all that Autumn recently told me a allegory?

When she first told me this, I was disoriented and liberated over it. I have no knowledge of medicine especially of those medical less alone technical advancements. I went through mom's library, and I could not find anything. I was hoping to find some medical or technical journals about it. Either this existed or it did not. I could not get anything on who helped. I mean, I was told friends and family of Autumn's connected to this system just for her.

This is a convoluted time paradox. Autumn was born long before I was. I somehow believe all she told me, but how? Was I this Sophia Bodhi before they gave me this title? There are too many questions and no answers, and it appears to me, the questions are multiplying.

I think the new name... wait a minute! It was named, esosophia before I was born — some time after I cured Autumn. She admitted to that. I need to know more what occurred that day... or how long it was when I was with her. I don't know. I am so befuddled. How it feels, we never departed. She contacted me some time after I cured her — I guess. This time thing is weird. It was like we were dear friends for years. If that monk is right, I have already fulfilled my duty, and I am doing it again — by curing every mind in this esosophia.

Talking about that Monk. His voice was... YES!! I remember he was Autumn's father. He wasn't a Neurosurgeon or help create the hive mind system. Let me think... if I remember right, he pleaded for help from the Neurosurgeons he knew.

NO!! What they created was me — Sophia. As the technology advanced, I became sentient. As Somova said, bits and pieces. Like when I was driving with mom the other day, it was a projection.

This... no... I was talking to myself. I am the same Sophia but I am not. OF COURSE!! Everyone has been calling me Sophia Bodhi. I feel like I am that same mind, but I have a unique life.

If that verse, Luke 12:48 was important, then I will be responsible for more than enlightenment. I surely don't want to be a religious figure or a Goddess for that matter; nevertheless, I asked daddy that question. Could it have been in my mind since I connected? I need to learn more. Could it be... NO WAY!! Autumn Heath is that me of that era. I don't believe it. I healed myself. This is becoming too much. I need to talk to Zak about this.

~~~~~

She did not finish reading it all, but she darted off before she would usually close any work she was doing. She had to talk to him.

When she was in the same room — the living room — not far from the dinning room, why is talking to you so important?"

He smiled warmly, "First, we all realized Autumn was either you or somehow related to you."

She looked more confused.

"It was all a show. Having you connected mentally to Autumn was as real as you and me, but apparently, what you were sharing with yourself was some complex metaphor."

She realized what her lover was telling her was the truth, but it was not Zak she had been knowing most of her life. She realized she was having a vision, still sleeping in her bed.

After forcing herself to wake up, "OH, MY! This is creepy. Will I know the difference between reality and this pseudo one?"

The voice of Autumn Heath said, "Yes, you will."

With a lot of confusion in her mind, she asked, "Are you me?"

"Yes, I am."
~~~~~

"How?"

"That is easy and complex. I had Rett Syndrome, but you cured me."

Sophia asked again, "How?"

"It is your nature to help others, but since you knew who I was... well not yet in your temporal understanding... you had to go to all lengths to cure me."

"Did I? I know you are healthy now, but this is confusing."

"Yes, you did."

"Let me see if I can get a handle on it. If I saved you, then how did the hive mind matrix start?"

"When you wrote, they created you, it was another metaphor, but it was 100% accurate."

"Good grief." She paused in thought, "are you saying when I was born, this mental system that tied everyone together was because of me? How?"

"Time was never linear. You curing me did not create some paradox as is in your brilliant mind."

"Are you referring that I created some sort of paradigm of my-self?"

"To your point of view, that would be correct. Stop trying to figure this out in the real since. As your daddy keeps saying to you, 'Philosophy of science without history of science is empty; history of science without philosophy of science is blind.' Stop trying to be so logical. You are blinding yourself by being too scientific."

Since Sophia could not say much more, she asked, "What does Zak have to do with this? Was that another metaphor?"

"Zak is your lover. Why he did not sound like himself is because you did not go to him as such."

Sophia thought she would lose her mind. What Autumn was saying got her confused the more.

"You did not run to him. It was a mental facsimile for one. Normally, you would not just dart off because you read his name somewhere."

Finally, she realized what she was wearing — her night clothes. "Good, I wore the proper clothing this time..." She froze is fear, "or is this another mental illusion?"

"No, silly willy."

They laughed

Sophia said, "I recalled I said that to you a lot."

"As Somova said, 'you are getting your memories in bits and pieces.' Usually, no one gets any from one's formal life."

"If I understand right, it is because of you."

She did not respond.

"How are we the same?"

"It is a complex answer."

"I bet."

"What you wrote down, they created you. That was the first true artificial intelligence that was fully sentient."

"I understand! They called her sophia because in the Greek it meant wisdom. I would have to guess, it found me sometimes after I connected."

"That is correct. In fact, we did. We became in all reality, one mind. That was how I was cured."

"Because I became that sophia, I ended up the one curing you?"

"Believe it or not, it was you. The A.I. could not do so alone. When I said, we found you, it was both a strong metaphor and real."

17

— • —

CHAPTER 16

The next morning, Sophia woke up, undressed, and went to the bathroom across the hall to take her morning shower.

When she went to her room to get dressed, she found her mother, as always, cooking breakfast. Pippa said with a warm smile, "Good morning."

At first she did not reply.

"Something wrong?"

"I was wondering if what we are saying is real?"

"Don't worry about that, baby."

Sophia sighed, "I would like to know."

"Like any mental exercise, you will need to focus on what you are doing. I mean, pay more attention to the details."

She told her mother what she had done recently, and how it is hard for her to know the difference.

"In time, you will get the hang of it. Like I told you when you thought you were driving with me. You could have easily have seen if that was a mental vision inside..." She hesitated, "inside what every one calls now, esosophia."

She plopped in her chair at the dining table, "Oh, bother!"

"Sweetie, you are not Winnie the Pooh."

Sophia laughed.

"This is a lot to deal with. I know I will make it, but... no I don't think I will make it." She paused, "I know I have done a great deal with my mind within this... okay, esosophia; nevertheless..."

Her father walked in the dining room and said, "You need to have more faith in yourself. Everyone else does." He paused, "I believe you have more faith in yourself then you are admitting. Why not try something different with exploring this matrix as you want to call it... despite what it should be called."

"Like what?"

"Explore what scares you... for one."

"What scares me... I was the one who cured Autumn, and I realized she is me at the same time. How?"

He thought for a moment, "Every discipline, philosophy, religion, and other walks of life has its own story about the creation of man. Which one do you believe?"

"What I have understood, the differences are based on many factors: cultures, the time it which that culture lived, and endless other things that makes each social class different even if their country is next door to another one."

He gave a noticeable grin, "Find out what is your way of life. This can only be answered by you, my daughter. If your duty has always been leading the human race on this esosophia, then you must know everything about yourself."

Sophia thought about it. She said, "Are you saying that Autumn Heath does not exist until I was born?"

Nikolas said, "Look at it without a linear concept. What you need to learn is not who was born first, or you may believe that you don't exist."

"Daddy, I know she exist. We have recently talked for hours. She wouldn't have said those things if she did not exist. She told me the A.I. could not cure her alone. That makes her real and this think tank that they called it, Sophia."

Pippa said, "It could be, but as you know, your name means wisdom. They could have called the first A.I. that. I have to believe that artificial intelligence is not really wise — at least not regarding human standards. People a long time ago were extremely arrogant."

Sophia said, "Yes, especially the early 21st century."

"We humans... some of them could... be that way. I think that is why they called our hive mind, esosophia. You made a difference for all of us, baby."

Noda Miyu appeared out of nowhere, "That is why I quickly changed my curriculum. Principle Lydia Day could not agree with me fast enough."

Sophia smiled, "When will I be able to report to my classes."

She gave her that stern look, "That is not what you are asking, young lady. You want to your old life back. In all you have done in adventuring in what will be called, esosophia... yourself."

She went wide eyed, "WHAT!? HOW!?"

"As your daddy had suggested, learn about yourself more." She paused, "once you start, you will not want to have your old life back." She paused again, "⊠⊠⊠⊠⊠⊠⊠⊠⊠⊠ (i no naka no kawazu taikai wo shirazu)"

She smiled, "A frog in a well knows nothing of the sea."

After Ms. Noda Miyu vanished, the Vitaloti family ate their breakfast and talked as all families do.

****

After Sophia did as she was told, she thought to check on her classmates and at the time of the Sociology Class. As always, she greeted Ms. Noda Miyu several minutes before the class started, "こんにちは (Kon'nichiwa.) / Good afternoon."

She smiled, "Good morning, Bodhi."

"Is it necessary for you to greet me by that name always?"

She gave Sophia a stern look, "No, but you are not supposed to be here."

"I know; I just wanted to checkout how everyone is doing... personally. As I would do if this... okay... Bodhi person never existed."

"Believe it or not, you existed before your biological body was born. Because you are ignorant of that, doesn't make it some form of mythology."

Yeva came into the classroom. DAMN IT, Sophia! Why are you here?"

She was perplexed how she knew she was there without having any image of her.

"The question running in your mind is easy. I have you nearly on my mind a lot... especially since you are part of the hive mind since the beginning. Do you think artificial intelligence could achieve this? Why did you think you asked your daddy that question? You cured Autumn sure enough, and it is easy why you, her, and this massive hive mind is all the same."

"SAY WHAT?! Are you pulling my leg?"

Noda Miyu said, "She doesn't need to do that. What you have created if you realize it or not while saving Autumn Heath's life came to a marvelous thing, and it has nothing to do with advanced technology."

Sophia suddenly appeared... not as a ghost, a hologram, or the like. She was there in the flesh. She sat down in her usual desk and said, "I am listening."

Yeva asked, "How did you do that?"

Sophia answered, "I am not really here. There is no way to transport my biological life to one location to the next."

"Talk to me, sweetie."

"Through this esosophia, I can create realistic illusions. I have done so with mom, Scarlet, and Zak. Through the same network, I can present myself in the same manner."

"That is freaking cool!"

As the students were gathering in, the instructor instructed everyone to take their seats. She continued, "We have an important guest with us." Sophia was about to protest, but Ms. Miyu stopped her, "don't be that way. You are after all a senior, and this year is about done. You have surpassed our standards, and your duty will have you to do more important things."

Yeva asked, "Does that mean I am some kind of royal ass kicker?"

Everyone laughed... including Sophia.

Sophia replied, "Kicking it and straighten it out are two different things."

Ms. Miyu said, "Yes, Yeva, you are responsible to get her to only behave, but support her in everything she will do." She paused, "now to continue where I left off. Having our minds connected is nothing special within itself. What you have created for all of humanity is a simple concept — UNITY OVER SELF. You asked your... Bampás that question because you felt that unity was dissolving."

Sophia gasped, "OH, MY, yes I did!"

Yeva said, "That is why we are supporting you, and why we all have called our hive mind — esosophia. Yes, your name means wisdom, and sweetie, you have shared you wisdom with us without bias, hatred, or the hype that the MAGA Trump's Republican Party had done eons ago."

A student said, "Why compare us with that screwy lunatic?"

Sophia answered, "I have been referring to that era because I am concerned we could be bias and the rest if we don't change our ways with our evolutionary status."

Ms. Miyu said, "That is why I changed my curriculum. There are a fair amount of others who has what Sophia is concerned about, but we are far from organized. Faith without works is not only a spiritual concept. It is a human one. That means the whole body of minds without unity in our esosophia is dead. It is why Sophia asked, "I am concerned why there are a good many that have not chosen to be connected to our hive." In reality, we can be connected while not by living in our comfort zone. As Neal Donald Walsch said, "life begins at the end of our comfort zone."

Sophia said, "I have been thinking lately if we are have caused that comfort zone to be an excuse to hide. I mean could it be that simple as to strip naked from all our clothing in a crowd of people and see each other for the first time. I wonder if that occurred, in less then five minutes, we would understand what it is to be human... this esosophia or not?"

Moments after she said, that she got the right cue from Ms. Miyu. Moments later she closed her eyes and she vanished. Seconds after, not only the classroom of students appears for the whole school body — in which they were monitoring the whole conversation.

Instead of wearing the clothing they were wearing on their bodies, they were completely naked as Sophia suggested.

It took about seven minutes for all of them to realize what she just stated was what they needed to administer. Of course it was not being mentally/physically naked that was the answer, but how simple a matter of what they were thinking now changed their perspective of how they thought. They wondered if they could easily keep that train of thought when they were in their bodies fully clothed.

Sophia said to them all, "I know this is only a first step. There will be billions upon billions upon billions of other steps. Don't worry, I don't expect you to be naked all the time, but I ask if we remember this moment as you continue to live your daily lives. You people are less then 1% of the populous of the world. I realized with all your multitude of believes, religions, and all the rest, it was hard for you to achieve this moment. I thank you."

Principle Lydia Day said, "It is us that should be thanking you."

Everyone cheered!

For the rest of the school day, all of them continued within their esosophia, naked. In fact, they did the same for nearly a week until the board of directors and the State government allowed them to be physically unclothed. Once word got out, it did not take long for the country and the whole State to take the plunged on what was shared with the others on what Sophia Vitaloti started without any physical or sexual hangups — as many were extremely nervous about occurring.

****

The next morning, Sophia was with her parents having breakfast. As they all were without a stitch on their bodies, she asked her daddy, "Did the Greeks go naked a lot in their time?"

He smiled, "Yes, they did. It is why their art had nudity. They believed nudity was a big part of human life. They respected it by their art and why the first Olympics were in the nude. After all gymnastics come from the Greek word, GYMNOS, which means naked or to strip."

"Naked or clothed, I am happy to be back in school. Yes, I know I am about to graduate this year, but I want to complete it. I wonder if I can continue being this inspiration of all in our hive mind... esosophia... if I did not?"

Pippa said, "I read that different States in the union are adopting our clothing social standards. It is not all of them, but a bit more than half of the nation."

Sophia thought — not looking at her parents for a moment, "I see in their minds they are starting to understand why I suggested this. She looked at them and continued, "as you have said, not all, but more and more are wanting to do so, and if I understand right, over a thousand has took the plunge today." She smiled after saying the last part.

"Your daddy and I are extremely proud of your accomplishments. I am sure you are excited to get back in school and all."

"Yes, I am. I miss the life I worked hard on before I started with knowing my duty of helping all with our hive mind system." She paused and sounded a bit nervous, "one small step for man, one giant leap for mankind."

Nikolas smiled, "Daughter, you have nothing to be fearful about. You have done a lot already for everyone. As you just felt, a lot are coming around what you have started. Don't be apprehensive of the ones who don't. They have the right to choose."

She smiled, "Yes, daddy, I know, and I don't want to rule others. The old novels about having a hive mind system like ours was not about..."

He interrupted, "Know this, you can't change the world, and you should not do that ever. Yes, those science fiction stories were silly, but what we are experiencing now is not. You are not, my lovely naked daughter."

"Thanks, daddy."

They continued to talk and eat breakfast as they usually do until they separated in their normal routines each day. As Sophia's mother was driving to Correlative Attentive High School, Sophia said, "I was tempted to mentally transport myself, but being away from school so long, I wanted to be in the flesh..." She laughed, "as it were."

"Baby, you started something that grew into a massive community. I would not be surprised if the rest of the world has not partaken in this."

"They have and at an alarming rate."

"What do you mean?"

"They could not denude themselves fast enough. It was why I asked daddy that question. Are we Americans still closed minded over nudity?"

After turning a corner, she smiled, "If most if not all of the people of our State has been naked — barely wearing shoes — then I say you have opened their minds up a lot more than you realized."

Sophia was so much absorbed by what she had done for not only the State she lived in, more than half of the people of the United States of America, but the entire world, she finally realized her mother was about to pull up to the front of the main building of the school. They said their normal goodbyes, and Sophia started to enter the building. When she saw The school Principal, she smiled, "Hello, Ms. Day. How are you?"

As the rest, she was fully undressed. There were more unclothed since that first mental adventure with Sophia. She replied, "It is great to see you Bodhi." Sophia was getting used to being called that. She smiled. Ms. Day saw this and continued, "Bodhi, in all I have seen enter this school building today and the campus, everyone and I mean everyone is completely naked because of what you started not too long ago."

"I was telling mom how fantastic the other nations have been doing just that. What I got from their minds, they could not denudify quick enough."

"I am not surprised at all. As I stated, everyone was mentally naked as if we were physically now. It took a while for the lawmakers to allow us to do so physically, but those things take time. I have to admit, they pushed it fast as if they could not disrobe fast enough." She paused, "please, don't concern yourself with those who can't or refuse to do so. You may never understand why, but that is life. Allow them to do so... whatever they choose."

"Now that I am more attuned to this esosophia, I have done so. At first, I thought I would be managing all sorts of minds, but I found out that it was not as bad as I thought."

She smiled, "Believe me, you had nothing to be concerned about. What I am getting from your mind, you simply feared what was your duty. Know this, Bodhi, each one of us has to live our purpose... one day at a time. I am sure you made mistakes and learned from them. That is life too."

She said in amazement, "Look at us. I know I was there for the duration, but everyone is naked as the day. What made me ask that question to daddy, and how can I make such an impact of the whole world."

"If you think all this is a dream, than stop right there. If it is as such, who is dreaming and who is not. Since this is everyone as you professed, no one is dreaming because this is real as life can get."

The two of them talked a bit before she had to get in her proper place to start the day. As she was walking to the right classroom, everyone cheered to say thank you for what she had done for them. The classmates and the instructor did the same thing. As suspected during the morning, each classroom did the same thing. Sophia was blessed that she had made a difference.

When she entered the lunchroom, she saw someone that was clothed. She was waiting for such people. She came close to him and introduced herself.

He smiled, "Hi, I am Josh Gallagher. Please have a seat."

"Thank you."

"After she sat down, he asked, "I take it you are interested in why I am clothed."

"That is none of my business, so you don't have to answer."

"I say, you are the first to address me in that manner."

"They all should." She realized Josh was not connected to the hive mind. It did not concern her, but she did experience something interesting about him as she first saw him sitting down at the table they both were sitting. She waited for him to take the initiative.

"You seem to be something important."

She smile slightly, "In all life, we are important."

She realized then and there he had no idea of the esosophia or anything about her then what she just told him. She said, "At least you are not disturbed in seeing so many unclothed or about why?"

"I learned from the media... you see I am not connected to this network. Anyhow, I learned that some individual, by the name Bodhi, somehow enlighten the world to see themselves stripped from their comfort zones. Maybe why I have not done so, I am not connected."

She studied him for a moment, quietly, and said, "Why would that make a difference? Do you want to be connected before you fully undressed?"

Josh thought for a moment, "Interesting question. I wonder if I am too old to start."

"There are many, many individuals that connected at different ages. I started at age nine."

"I thought nearly everyone connected at birth."

She gave a warm smile, "Not at all. Everyone has choices in life. That includes connecting or not. No one will force you to do so... including me."

He sighed in relieve. He asked, "How does one connect if it is not done at birth or something?"

"The technology is simple. It is through nanobots. To really understand unity over self is another manner."

He looked a bit serious, "What is that... I mean... I know what you said, but I did not realize it was that dynamic." He paused, "I think that is the right word for it."

"Actually, the right word would be... esosophia."

"Wait a minute. Your name is Sophia. Are you telling me you are this matrix or whatever?"

"What I have learned, but it is more complex than that, but yes, I am the one you speak. Know this: it is not because of my name as the sake of me. Sophia means in the Greek, wisdom."

"Don't cut yourself short. You saw something in me, and it is more than me being fully dressed."

"Yes, you have interested me, but I stand by what I said. What you do... naked or not... is completely up to you. I understood the State governments have made that crystal clear, and I made sure they gave everyone the right to be connected to our... esosophia."

He just smiled.

"I was told by Principal Day, everyone was naked. It seemed we all missed someone, so please let me introduce myself again. I am Sophia (Bodhi) Vitaloti."

Josh gave a warm smile, "It is great to meet you, Bodhi. I take it that it is more of a title of royalty than awakening or enlightenment?"

Yeva came up to them. She said, "A royal pain in the ass." She laughed.

Sophia replied, "She is my court jester."

He laughed and said, "At least you two are close friends."

Yeva introduced herself. "Sorry, I did not formally introduce myself in class earlier."

"No problem. I am Josh Gallagher, and I am new. Since this semester started not too long ago, I guess they allowed me to start. I am able to catch up on things a lot later than this. It is why I really didn't want to join this hive mind network."

Sophia realized Zak wasn't anywhere on campus.

Yeva caught her be concerned and said, "Zak is fine. I will tell you about it, later."

Josh said, "Zak is your..."

Yeva interrupted, "Yes, her boyfriend."

Sophia scolded her for interrupting. She had a constant habit in doing that."

"There is no problem, and I am more comfortable in seeing nudity than you may realize. My family were nudists... and still are, but I am not."

"As I said, Josh, you are free to decide. What you heard about me getting everyone to do so, it was first in the esosophia. It was a while before the governments allowed everyone to do so physically. Please don't do so on our account."

"In knowing how genuinely friendly and the rest, I was starting to feel I could do so. Before he could say, 'I could put my clothes in my book bag, he started to undress.

Josh said, "How do I connect to this esosophia?"

18

EPILOGUE

School went on for several days, and it was a blessing. Sophia was enjoying being back. She enjoyed learning, and helping the other students when it was needed of her. Most importantly, she felt great to be back in what she was doing before she new she was this Bodhi.

It wasn't like she did not enjoy that too, but she wanted her life back. It was hers, and she need to complete high school. She was not a quitter and if she could not do so, she would have believed she had failed somehow. Even if she created this hive mind network, she had to complete her schooling. She did not want to be considered a dropout. Every aspect of her life so far had been important to her.

If she was to be some kind of hierarchy within this esosophia, being the best she could be is just as meaningful. She had experienced a great deal of her duty within meditating within this network. She believed she learned a great deal about herself in ways she did not expect.

After her time with Ms. Miyu's class that day as a holographic persona of herself, she really got the world thinking and believing in themselves not by going completely physically naked, but from within themselves. When she mentioned that, she did not expect them to even undress in the esosophia matrix. After more than half the nation and parts of the world initially undressed in public life, she was astounded on what she had accomplished.

Sophia was dumbfounded that more took the plunge in something they had never done in their lives — lived as they were meant to live. There is an importance in wearing clothing. The environment was still in a fickle over this global warming. As predicted in the early 21st century, things became extremely chaotic, but nothing were dying as they thought. All the lifeforms adapted including humanity.

No matter the weather and the environment, everyone opened up more — being fully naked. It appeared everyone at the school was enjoying themselves. Since Josh Gallagher was new — at least to her — she quietly checked up on her through the esosophia. "WOW! He does adapt quickly. I must meed his parents since he said they were nudists. I would have already met them and not know it. Why am I worried over him anyhow. I need to stop this. I keep saying I refuse to live for others. Josh is a person I have barely met, but he did interest me on that first day I met him." She decided to focus on something else.

While sitting alone at one of the tables in the lunchroom, she thought to check on Zak.

He caught her doing so. He said, "I am on assignment... part of the Sociology class project."

"I thought as much. With no one telling me about it, I thought you were at the State Capitol talking to the Governor."

"WOW! You are good."

"Maybe, but where else would you be. How is it going?"

"Slow. I can't know at this time if we are making progress or not. Several other students are with me from the government class. Ms. Miyu knew these students have talked to our Governor before."

"When am I needed?" "Dammit! I am doing it again — over worrying about things. I see in Zak's mind, he knows what he is doing, and he hasn't told me all that much. I need to chill, or I will drive myself crazy."

"For now, stay in school. From checking up on you and having your mother talk to me, you need to be there."

She sighed in relief in her mind, but did not allow him to notice, "True, but I want to be with you, too."

"When are you not an opened book to me. There is nothing to fear, and it is why we have not told you hardly anything. There is a lot to share, but you are too wound up, so I will not say anymore." He said to her, "I know, and I feel the same way."

"Do I need to talk to anyone?"

"These meetings are to design just that. We may have others around the nation to join us."

"WOW! That soon. I was expecting everyone to gather but WOW!"

"What I have heard from a reliable source, more State governments want to allow their people to go stark naked as we are, but they want to meet you first in person. Apparently they knew your past."

"I don't understand how, but a lot have here. While at the same time, they did not know it when they first knew me."

"I have to admit, love, I am perplexed by that too." He paused, "you better finish eating lunch and finish your school day. Talk with you later. I love you."

"I love you, too."

When she opened her eyes, there were Yeva and Somova sitting at the same table.

Somova asked, "How is Zak?"

She told them about the conversation.

Yeva said, "We kept that from you so you would not worry."

She smiled, "Thanks."

Somova asked, "So you will be talking to all the elected officials of every State."

"I doubt everyone."

"Trust me,you will talk to a great deal. I am sure only a few will be at our Capitol in person, the rest will be there through our technologies."

Sophia replied, "No Internet video conferencing could group that many either. I think it will be up to me to find away for all to communicate around the nation if not the world."

Yeva said, "You are super intelligent, girl, but you are not that good."

Somova said, "They had Governor conferences before. They would know how to gather people."

"From how Zak felt, I think this will be something unique. I know I have talked to endless minds at once when I was flexing my muscles as it were. There may be more than Governors at this meeting."

"What makes you think that?"

After having another bite of her lunch she said, "Think about it. Most if not all at the school is naked at the day. I have been having a great deal of people thanking me in this esosophia by having more States laws allowing them to be naked too." She paused a bit after finishing her meal. "they are doing the work. Yes, I had a big influence, but I am at the moment not doing a damn thing."

They both smiled. Yeva said, "That is why we have been keeping quiet about Zak talking to the governments all over the nation. We thought they would only thank you for what you started here at this school. You have done more than even I have realized."

Somova said, "That is the real definition of our Constitutional Federal Republic. The government should not do as much as they had done during the 20th and 21st centuries. Because of our comfort zones in our esosophia — until you had made a difference here lately..."

"You mean I was and wasn't the creator of this?"

Autumn Heath appeared — naked at they were — as a hologram of sorts sitting at their table. She said, "My sister..."

Sophia cried out, "WHAT?!"

"We are mental sisters..."

"OH, MY! I remember we said that to each other a lot. I also remember we were naked a lot when I was with you."

She smiled, "Yes, we were. I always loved my physical body, and after I was being cured of my Rett Syndrome, I could function a lot more as I progressed." She paused, "you did not create anything other than the minds that you are doing now." She paused for a moment and continued, "let me explain. You were the influencer of starting this mental network with the neighbors. Their healthy genome cured my body more than anything. It is more than their minds connected, but you allowed them to reprogram my genome. From there more and more wanted to connect. It is a great deal to go into, but as the old saying, 'the rest is history.' I have my sister to thank, for curing me."

"Any time love."

Yeva said, "I am not a bit surprised in hearing this, and I would expect what you shared with us is not the highlight of what she had done."

Autumn looked at her and said, "Yes, she had done so much more that a mere history book could not explain."

Sophia asked, "How come?"

"My sister, in a lot of ways, it has not happened yet while at the same time a lot have been accomplished."

"Are you saying what is going on today will occur in your time?"

"In order to get a handle on this you must not think of it as time... I mean linear time. Just live your life at this moment. Remember, the journey is more important than the destination."

Somova said, "That is why Zak did not want us to tell you what he is doing. Trust me love, he has not revealed that much on what he was doing."

"I thought so, but I could not prove it."

"Don't try to figure it out, either. Allow things to come to you in their own merits. Besides, you are in school..." the bell went off. "and you should concentrate on that."

"My sister, you will do great. Hurry up... you don't want to be late in being early to Ms. Miyu's class." She vanished.

As usual, Sophia was on time in being early. In fact, she was a few minutes earlier.

"□□□□□□□□□□□(Mi yu-san, kon'nichiwa.) / Good afternoon, Ms. Miyu."

She smiled at Sophia, "□□□□□□□□□□ □□□□□□□□□ (Kon'nichi-wa, Bodi. Kyō wa genkidesu ka?) Good afternoon, Bodhi. How are you, today?"

Bodhi spoke in English, "I am doing great. I had a small talk with Zak while I was eating lunch."

She was quiet for a short time, but for Sophia's observation skills, it lasted longer. Ms. Miyu said, "There is more that is going on than you realize. It is why I got the other students to be with him."

She squinted.

Ms. Miyu saw that and replied, "You will not get anything from me, young lady."

When she said that, it meant the conversation was at an end. Sophia took her seat politely and quietly.

Not too long, the other students gathered in... naked as everythi ng... because of Bodhi — their enlightenment. Sophia saw that and smiled warmly.

As expected, this class day, they did not get into the project. Sophia was disappointed, but she tried not to show it.

Autumn said in her mind, "My sister, behave yourself. You are more than royalty to them. At least, they will show you that if you are royalty or not. You should act like it."

"I know that, sister. I take it that is what Zak and the others are doing?"

"You will not get a peep out of me."

She shared a warm feeling, "Good."

Ms Miyu said, "Even though you know sociology started in the 19th century by Auguste Comte, it crudely started much earlier. Confucius started to recognized social behaviors in the 13th century; it was the same with Ma Duanlin. Since civilizations has been flourishing many throughout the ancient era, in which we call 'lost civilizations,' people could have been studying social behaviors since the dawn of civilization. Today, we have many, many disciplines to allow us to do that even Auguste could not have dreamed."

She looked at Sophia, "As we are now starting to realize Bodhi had started our hive mind network that we suddenly been calling, esosophia. I have to admit, things are starting to wake up — for all of us." She made herself look at the students, "I can't say if we will learn things that we never understood before, but know this, whatever is in store, nothing bad has happened to us." She looked at her again, "that means you, Princess Bodhi."

Sophia blurted out, "PRINCESS?! What are you talking about?"

Every student gave her a roaring cheer.

Sophia was about to cry for joy.

Ms. Noda Miyu smiled.

Yeva said teasingly, "Since Somova and I are her best friends, Ms. Miyu, it may be required for you to ordain us to be the royal ass kicker."

Everyone laughed including Sophia. She said to Yeva, "Так звичайно. Якщо ви не могли цього зробити раніше, чому ви думаєте, що можете зараз? (Tak zvychayno. Yakshcho vy ne mohly ts'oho zrobyty ranishe, chomu vy dumayete, shcho mozhete zaraz?) / Yeah, right. If you could not do it before, why do you think you can now?"

Since everyone, through the esosophia understood every word she said, they all answered in unison, "We love you, that is why?"

Sophia could not stop her tears of love from streaming down her face. She suddenly realized how much she made a difference. She didn't understand the nonlinear time aspect, but right now, that did not matter.

The rest of the school day went quick. Sophia was in an euphoria state until her mother drove them both home.

****

After arriving home after a full school day, she gathered herself in her room. She mediately sat down at her desk, and she turned on her computer. Instead of writing papers for the class project, she ended up writing a journal. Sophia had to write down all that was going on. Actually, she had started one already.

~~~~~

OH, MY GOD! I am still on cloud nine over what they did for me in Ms. Miyu's class. I have never had that much love from so many people in such a giant way — if that can describe it. I don't think no word or words could.

I have to admit, a great deal is going on. Deep in my soul, I have realized this, but until now, I could not get myself to admit it. The why is easy. I was scared out of my mind. In a lot of ways, I still am. How can this happen to me. How can asking daddy that question make such an impact?

It has done so just the same. I am no savior, but at the same time, I am still saving the minds that want to be enlightened. In all the help I have given students at the school before I realized I was this Bodhi, I just simply realized that I could help them help themselves. My sister was right. I helped her family connect to this esosophia for her benefit. Today, I realized the minds that were connected were developing into their comfort zones that I believe had caused the individuals that were not a part of this network to be pushed out. That meant both were in danger.

Because of me, there are safe, but the journey still continues. What is scaring me now, what am I supposed to do? Could we have
~~~~~

politicians screw up this hive mind matrix? Or will they help every-one achieve their very best. General Patton once said, "Individuality is a bunch of horse dung." The masses can't get out of their comfort zones if we fight each other like what had occurred with Donald J. Trump. That Pandora's box is still open, and we can have this start all over again with so much division I wonder anyone can stop.

Yes, I am over worrying again. There has been no type of activity like that within our esosophia. Like my girl friends have said, I would have worried over this, so I better stop before I really get started. If the worse does happen, right now, there is nothing I can do about it.

Come to think of it, why should I not be concerned. I have done a lot lately. SIGH!! Everyone would know I have, and would be overly concerned. I need to chill if I am going to apply things in the right way. I am sure these government leaders will test my resolve. Some may do so to see if I can deal with this, and many would have already believe I could or should not do this at all. Nudity is still a scary subject for most in the United States, but they have all realized what I stated and proving me right.

They are only doing the work because of what I have gotten them to think and believe. I know that now. There is more to be done. We all will do it — together.

~~~~~

Autumn said in her head, "Do you know what you think you know?"

"I am learning more regarding, but I could never be fully pre-pared."

"That is a healthy response. You were always weak on self-confi-dence."
~~~~~

"Hell! What do you expect. This is the whole population of the world. Since they don't do population census anymore, it is hard to know how many are living."

"That would not matter anyhow. Nearly everyone looks up to you."

"Come on! I would expect less than half are paying attention to me."

"When I say nearly everyone, sister, I mean everyone."

"How do you know that?"

"I know you. In how you started my family and neighbors to connect to help cure me, I believe it is the rippling effects how how so many are connected today."

Sophia realized she was right. She could not gather any count, but every soul she had encountered — including the ones that recently showed their gratitude — it was an extremely high amount. It is like they were telling her how many without an actual number. All that mattered is she was the one that was responsible.

****

As Sophia's boyfriend and soon to be husband, Zak Harris is setting a journey that will fulfill her life far more than she can envision. She has done a great deal already. It is not just getting people all over the world to go without any clothing, but the finally shedding of taboos, false moralities, and the corrupt industrial standards that has plagued humanity even before the Industrial Age began.

The thriving of the evolution of humanity is not necessarily technical, medical, and other wonders, but the standards of the human mind. Today, we are advancing with artificial intelligence but we are not doing so with ourselves. Because in Sophia's era, linking the human mind through some advanced A. I. doesn't necessarily advance civilization. When Bodhi truly speaks the every leader and every individual, that will present the spark of collecting a new era of Homo sapiens all around the world.

Today, we don't need to undress or have our minds connected to some hive network to do the same. All we have to do is learn the honor code that will achieve greatness. What that means, we start to live the highest standard we can possibly live — through ourselves, a community, a nation, and humanity itself. It does not forcing others who they can love, what rights certain people can have, or what others believe. It is teaching that we can live, love, etc. any way we please while tolerating the differences we may not like. Laws are to serve and protect — never to control certain groups.

Ms. Noda Miyu called Sophia Princess for a reason, and the student body of that class accepted it, so have the other human minds all around the world. There will be a lot of work for our Princess to do, but she can't do it alone. Humanity is not meant for everyone to be hermits. We are to work together and make the best in life. General Patton said, "An army is a team. It lives, eats, sleeps, fights as a team. This individuality stuff is a bunch of crap. The bilious bastards who wrote that stuff about individuality for the Saturday Evening Post don't know anything more about real battle than they do about fornicating."

Humanity today do not need to connect their minds to live, eat, sleep, and fight for what makes our nation great as a Constitutional Federal Republic. Throughout human history, the majority will always fall into a comfort zone. That is why Sophia asked her Bampás that question. It wasn't the question in itself that sparked things from everyone within this esosophia, but why she asked it. Sometimes a small spark can create a big fire. Bodhi means enlightenment, and Sophia means wisdom.

She lived up to both expectations, and she has not started on what she can do. There is a lot for our protagonist to do, and it could take several stories before it is over. Think of this story as a barely a preamble. There will be much more to come as each story continues.

www.ingramcontent.com/pod-product-compliance
Lightning Source LLC
Chambersburg PA
CBHW070952180726
48291CB00004B/1250